CHILD OF GABRIEL

The Battle for the Lost Amulet

A. M. Raithatha

instant apostle

First published in Great Britain in 2015

Instant Apostle
The Barn
1 Watford House Lane
Watford
Herts
WD17 1BJ

British Library Cataloguing-in-Publication Data

A catalogue record for this book is available from the British Library

This book and all other Instant Apostle books are available from Instant Apostle:

Website: www.instantapostle.com

E-mail: info@instantapostle.com

ISBN 978-1-909728-36-3

Printed in Great Britain

About the author

Anne Maria Raithatha co-wrote *BBA and Proud* which won an Edinburgh Fringe First in 2000 and then the children's TV series *My Life as a Popat* which won a BAFTA in 2005. Today Maria teaches science and maths at one of England's top prep schools.

Look out for the other books in the *Child of Gabriel* series.

Manoj, Chandni, Ishaan, Alice, Joshua and Micah.

Thank you to my family and friends.

For all the forgotten children.

Contents

Contents

Chapter 1
Devil Girl

As he leaned towards her, Kenya noted he had an unnecessary amount of aftershave that was fighting a battle with his body odour. She dared not turn away, as that often resulted in prolonging his rhetoric.

'You're useless! Just like your old man,' he bellowed.

Her lack of emotion appeared to anger him further.

'Just… Just get out of my sight!' he stuttered, obviously struggling to find an insult to fire at the glaring rock of a girl standing in front of him.

'If you shut your eyes then I will be out of your sight,' muttered Kenya under her breath.

'What did you say, gal? Don't you answer me back, devil gal!'

He moved suddenly to grab her but she already knew his routine and dodged in time, sending him stumbling into the kitchen table, knocking over the piled-up plates and takeaway containers that had made their home there. With all his energy he lunged at the girl, catching her flailing arm. He raised his hand in line with her face and brought it down with a swift action. Kenya braced herself but the pain did not materialise. She opened her eyes to see her mother holding the hand of her stepfather.

'What has she done this time? You let the devil wind you up, Dermott!'

Ardenne stared long and hard at Kenya. In contrast to her daughter, Ardenne was an elegant, well-dressed woman. Her chiselled bone structure was so fine that a statue of her would not look out of place gracing a drawing room on a country estate. She moved with such fluidity; ready to pounce on anyone who dared to question her. Such was the power of her beauty, it masked the ugliness of her heart to all. All except Kenya.

Ardenne was a formidable woman who ruled with an iron fist. If any slapping was to be done, then she would do it. Kenya knew that her mother had convinced herself that her frequent beatings of her daughter were not carried out because of malice, but to ensure the 'devil girl' did not end up like her 'wayward' father.

'Damn it, Ardenne. She, she, she... makes me do it! She just stands there staring at me,' blubbered her husband.

Ardenne stroked Dermott on the back as if he were a sick spaniel, whilst directing Kenya with a tut and a stabbing point from her bejewelled finger. Kenya knew the routine. She only had limited time in order to finish her homework each day before her mother returned from work. Piled on one of the kitchen work surfaces was

Kenya's science project, taunting her in all its incompleteness. Dermott had managed to cover her once-pristine notes in a mixture of Guinness Punch and greasy fingerprints. Kenya sighed heavily, stuffing her crumpled homework into the cupboard under the sink. Seething with quiet anger, she knew she would have to take yet another day off school to avoid facing detention. With heavy heart , Kenya put the kettle on and brought out her mother's 'joy' – a floral Cath Kidston-esque cup and matching biscuit tin; a delicate contrast to Ardenne's gruff manner.

The kitchen was Kenya's workroom. The once white units were now a vomit yellow with streaks of dried-on hot chilli sauce embedded into the crevices and grooves. The grimy oven was caked in years of grease that was impenetrable to Kenya's scrubbing and every cleaning product tried. Kenya's routine included mopping the vinyl floor every morning, only for it to return to its sticky norm within minutes of Dermott returning from work. Kenya often thought the man was so slimy that he oozed the gooey residue as he wandered around the kitchen.

As Kenya neatly arranged the biscuits on a plate, her parents spoke about her as if she was not there.

'I don't like that girl mixing with the old woman,' said Dermott, kicking the takeaway containers into the corner of the kitchen before sitting down in front of his wife.

Whenever the phrase 'old woman' was used, Kenya knew they were speaking about her beloved grandmother, Adosia. When Darcus and Ardenne had finally split, so had Kenya's connection with her nan. Ardenne had taken great pleasure in stopping her from seeing Adosia. Kenya pondered the reason behind her mother's change of heart after three painful years of separation.

'What if she talks? I swear the devil will tell her to talk,' continued Dermott. Dermott was a wiry man whose limbs hung loosely from his thin frame. His meagre body was in contrast to his pride and joy – a symmetrical afro that stood proudly on his head. The look was finished with a signature red plastic afro comb wedged firmly in his hair. No amount of schooling could alter Dermott's natural affinity towards stupidity. His foolish pursuits were known by all who had the misfortune to spend more than five minutes in his presence. Confusion reigned when anyone tried to fathom why a bright, sharp woman such as Ardenne would choose Dermott as a partner. Kenya often thought the huge plot of land held by Dermott's frail mother in Jamaica helped form their 'love union'. In her eyes, Ardenne was more suited to Dermott than she had been to her father, Darcus.

Ardenne and Darcus were chalk and cheese. There were always disagreements between them, so it was difficult for Kenya to recall just when their marriage had started to break down. It was fair to say, she thought, that it was always in a state of repair.

Once she had given Kenya's father his marching orders, Ardenne made it difficult for him to see Kenya. Long-held agreements on access would be changed with a moment's notice. Kenya knew Ardenne's actions were not borne out of misplaced love or concern for her. She was a mere pawn to her mother – nothing more than a valuable bargaining tool and a source of revenue. Over time, Ardenne's whispered tales of Darcus' neglect of his family spread around the neighbourhood. When he finally lost his finance job in the city, Ardenne's tales gained validity.

As Kenya got to work on reducing the precarious pile-up in the kitchen sink, she was reminded of Jenga. Like the game, she didn't dare to remove a dirty plate lest it cause an avalanche of dishes to break in the process. Kenya reflected that her fragile life was just like Jenga too. One false move and her world would cave in.

As Ardenne wittered on about her daughter's 'laziness', Kenya found that the monotonous movements of her soapy hands scrubbing crockery lulled her away to revisit the echoes of her past. The time when Ardenne's plans to find a new husband came sharply into focus.

Ardenne and her friends often consulted mediums and fortune tellers to seek guidance and cast spells on those who had wronged them. It was the first time Ardenne had used this woman, who was hidden away in a back alley in the town centre. Kenya had been dragged along in the hope that the medium would drive out the demons inside her as 'a freebie'.

Kenya and Ardenne had entered a womb-like room with thick red carpets covering the wall space. The heavy scent of patchouli curled its way around the room from several smouldering incense sticks. Kenya placed her hand over her mouth to stifle a choking cough as the incense plumes hit the back of her throat. Through the haziness of the room, they saw a motionless elderly woman on a large wing-back chair. Ignoring her guests, her eyes remained closed in deep meditation. The circular wooden table in front of her took up most of the remaining space in the room. To her side, a large paraffin lamp provided the heat and the only light. Though she must have been in her eighties, the face of the elderly woman was supple, with a youthful glow. Her head was covered with a large cloth and rose to a height above her. Yards of a colourful wrap were bound around her large frame, with a contrasting blouse peeking through.

When the woman eventually opened her eyes, Kenya felt her mother jump slightly in her chair. Her brown eyes surveyed Ardenne slowly before she spoke.

'Welcome, Ardenne. Welcome to Sister Brown's home,' she whispered gently, whilst holding out her hand for payment. As if on cue, Ardenne brought out from her shopping bag an envelope stuffed with money and a plastic wallet of items. Kenya looked on astonished as her mother handed over one of Darcus' old pay receipts, a set of his cufflinks and a small photo of him. The medium began her set, chanting numerous incantations and burning each of the items in the lamp's flames. The longer it proceeded, the more fearful Kenya became. The incense, the heat and the chanting was becoming unbearable, and then the woman stopped as quickly as she had started.

'You will find your pot of gold soon,' she smiled at Ardenne. 'And a man with money, my dear. Money!'

'Finally!' Ardenne exclaimed triumphantly. 'I'm sick of scraping by 'cos of this noose around my neck!' It took Kenya a while to register that her mother was referring to her as the hangman's tool. Sister Brown cast a long look at the girl and gave Ardenne a sympathetic nod.

'I deserve this promised money. The good Lord knows I deserve a happy, long life, Sister Brown,' she added with a sorrowful sound to her voice.

Ardenne was an open book. All too easy to read for Kenya. She was capable of turning on a river of tears or contorting her face into the most heartbroken of expressions within seconds. Kenya knew this promise of money was good news for her mother. Time and time again she would snarl at her, saying, 'The only good thing 'bout you is the size of your inheritance!' Could the medium's revelation be pointing to the death of her beloved grandmother? The death of Darcus' mother could not come soon enough for Ardenne. Sadly, Kenya

17

concluded that her mother's happiness lay in her own misery.

Impatiently, Ardenne drummed her fingernails on the table. 'When will I get this...?' she questioned.

'Beware!' interrupted Sister Brown, her voice shrill. 'The light from her will stop you in your tracks. She will stop you! Time to go! Time to go!'

Sister Brown jumped up quickly, as if her chair were on fire. The lamp and the table wobbled as she gestured wildly to Ardenne and Kenya to leave.

Sister Brown continued to screech 'Beware!' to Ardenne as they stood on the pavement outside. As Ardenne neatened her coat, Sister Brown gave Kenya a long, deadly stare which penetrated to her very core. Ardenne was not listening any more. She was far away, thinking out loud about what to spend Kenya's inheritance on as well as finding her 'Mr Moneybags'.

'Beware!' Sister Brown hissed before disappearing through her door once more. Ardenne paid no heed to the medium's warnings, but Kenya pondered them in her heart.

After this, Ardenne had gone on to book her annual short trip around the Caribbean, which comprised six weeks away from 'that troublesome gal'. Kenya did not mind at all as she spent those blissful weeks with Adosia. However, far from her sight, a twisted form of fate and not love caused Ardenne's eyes to meet Dermott's in a hotel bar in the Blue Mountains in Jamaica.

Dermott was the youngest child of a wealthy family on the island. His forefathers had pooled their money to open a loan company. They lent money to dirt-poor farmers who could not get a mortgage from a bank. Their wealth quickly grew as they benefited by seizing land from payment defaulters as well as earning high interest on their loans. Dermott's three sisters had continued in the family business as well as accumulating more wealth through marriage.

However, things were different for Dermott. From an early age it was obvious he did not possess the same financial skills, wit and intelligence as his sisters. He despised learning and was very wary of girls smarter than himself. He became increasingly spiteful towards his sisters, who were constantly praised by all outside the home. Luckily, being the only male in his family meant he 'got by', safe in the knowledge that he would fare better in the inheritance stakes. Spoilt by his widowed mother, Dermott secured an easy job of overseeing the highly competent managers on the family's coffee estate. It was a job that involved him doing nothing in which he was an expert.

However, one thing saddened his mother – the lack of a decent woman in his life. Fed up with the lack of suitable ladies, he decided one day to attend a dinner and dance in a hotel not far from Port Antonio. No one was more beautiful than the elegant woman from London at the bar. Here he fell deeply in love with Ardenne the first time he saw her, and she with him – once she had worked out the size of his inheritance.

Dermott never trusted Kenya. She had that look of intelligence that Dermott had battled against with his sisters. No way was he going to let that girl run rings round him.

His eyes tracked Kenya as she placed the cup and biscuits in front of her mother. Without thinking, he leaned over to grab one of Ardenne's prized shortbread biscuits. Swiftly, with the deadly precision of a ninja master, Ardenne slapped Dermott's hand, sending the biscuit flying back onto the plate. She carried on her conversation as if nothing had occurred, whilst Dermott clutched his hand in pain. Stirring her tea, she quietly reassured her husband, 'She will not say anything. Remember, the old woman is ill. And old women have a habit of leaving their "will and testament" to sick animals!' Smiling at her own joke she continued, 'And there is no animal as sick as that!' pointing at Kenya.

Dermott remained silent until the penny dropped, then laughed heartedly. 'Sick animals, yeah,' he repeated, sneering at Kenya.

Stupid fool, thought Kenya. She had little respect for the man – a mere lapdog to her mother. He hadn't a thought in his head unless Ardenne put it there, and a backbone only when Ardenne was present, and even then you could not really class him as a vertebrate. Kenya knew Dermott was Ardenne's 'pot of gold' as promised by Sister Brown. However, Ardenne hadn't reckoned on meeting her match in Dermott's wily mother. The sharp-thinking widow had continued to build on the fortune left to her by her late husband and was not prepared to give up her wealth to a gold-digging Ardenne. Kenya smiled as she remembered her mother screaming in fury when she found out that Dermott's mum had locked away the majority of her son's share of the money left by his father to avoid him squandering cash on his devious new bride. Kenya's mother was left to dream about future fortunes she could gather by the death of Adosia instead.

'That old hag owes me! When Darcus left me, she didn't give me a penny. She just sits in that old house taking up space.'

'Don't you fret, Ardenne. The old gal will soon be dead and then we can par-ty hard.'

Dermott rose from his seat to do an impromptu dance, slipping on a half-eaten chicken leg on the floor.

Kenya quickly stifled a laugh, turning away sharply towards the sink.

'Get this pit tidied up. Move, nah!' shrieked Dermott as he threw a dirty container at Kenya. She dodged, causing the contents to splatter across the kitchen wall in front of her. Kenya drew in a breath ready to respond, but a dark look from Ardenne caused her to rethink.

21

'Get it tidied up,' said Ardenne in a low voice.

Kenya sighed as she picked up her broom. Even Cinderella got a break to go to the ball.

Chapter 2
Longley Road

Sandwiched between two larger terraces on either side, the house on Longley Road where Kenya lived was so narrow it looked as if it had been built as an afterthought. Once Darcus' pride and joy, the front garden was now home to opportunistic weeds which sprung up through the uneven patio slabs. The once-neat border of rose bushes had turned yellow, fighting for nutrients with large nettles and bindweed.

Some years before, Kenya's father had cleared a space in the front garden of their home in Harrow for his young daughter. During those joyful moments, her weekends would be spent laughing and working on 'Kenya's patch'. Each year a riot of tulips in spring would give way to a summer of gladioli standing to attention. But now, like the laughter, the plants were dead and gone, buried under a water-damaged headboard on which Dermott's rusty scooter sat.

Propped up against the collapsing fence lived an old stained mattress which reeked to high heaven of every tomcat in the vicinity. Dermott had attempted to resolve the issue by pinning a car air-freshener to the offending item. Therefore, visitors waiting on the doorstep were subjected to the gut-wrenching smell of urine mixed with a cheap pine scent. Equally uninviting was a hastily handwritten note stating 'doorbell nah work' that was stuck to the weathered door. The indigo paint that Darcus had used for the front door was so faded that Kenya only had memories of its former grandeur. The front of the house whispered to Kenya of past glories of beauty and happiness. Each time she returned to the house, her heart sank a little lower than before.

Two rooms led off from the downstairs hallway. The front room was a monument to Ardenne. It was exclusively for visitors and out of bounds to Kenya, who often braved a yelling to sneak a look inside. Two long, plump sofas were squeezed into the room, along with an oversized floral armchair. Both were covered with a thin plastic sheeting which produced amusing sounds when occupied. A set of mock Queen Anne nesting tables occupied the small inner space on top of a shagpile rug. A glass-fronted sideboard ran the length of one wall, a showcase for Ardenne's cut-glass trinkets. The geometric wallpaper was interspaced with glossy photos of Ardenne and Dermott's frequent trips abroad. The rectangular stains left from the frames containing Darcus and Kenya's photos were still present, no matter how hard Dermott made Kenya clean the walls. It was a source

24

of annoyance for Ardenne. Traces of her ex-husband had to be eliminated.

Kenya was allowed into the TV room, if only to clean it. The central feature of this room was Dermott's 36-inch plasma TV complete with Bose surround sound system, which was shoehorned into an already cluttered room. This was the dumping ground where Dermott cast off his jackets, boots and food leftovers. This was his domain, though Ardenne blamed all the mess and bad smell on Kenya's 'laziness'. Dermott lived the bachelor life in this room with Kenya on call when his 'spars' crawled out of the woodwork with the promise of football and rum. The kitchen, therefore, was the only room downstairs which Kenya had permission to be in, and then only to fulfil her parents' wishes.

Marginal freedom was found in the damp back room upstairs which was Kenya's bedroom. It was in contrast to that of her parents, who occupied the large master room at the front of the house. Kenya's room was her world. Ardenne remarked that she would catch a disease spending any time in that squalid room, and therefore usually sent Dermott in to bark on her behalf. The fact that the room was unpleasant to her parents made it special for Kenya.

Though a depressing cloud rested heavily on the house, Kenya's room gave her light; it was a safe haven for her 'hidden treasures', a small collection of mismatched broken items deemed by Ardenne not important enough to be repaired. A small wine box with a dainty crocheted doily was her bedside table. Her camp bed was covered by a single patchwork blanket made by her grandmother. Kenya would often stand on her creaking bed to look out of the old sash window at people wandering by in the evening. Occasionally, the lonely look of this girl caught the eye of a passer-by, causing an embarrassed Kenya to dart behind the old bed sheet of a curtain which hung across the window frame.

It did not make sense, hiding from the world, allowing only the glare of the street light from across the road to look down on her. At night-time, the lamp's silhouette would fall onto the floor in the centre of the room. Here the floorboards were covered with a small rag rug in summer, with the addition of old newspapers in winter. If Ardenne were ever to have dared to look around the room she may have moved the rug and found an uneven floorboard. A closer inspection would have revealed that the floorboard could be removed. In this space, Kenya stored her 'most precious': a photo of herself and her father. Often she would stroke the smiling picture. The background was a party at a family friend's home. Kenya had long forgotten who.

There had been so many gatherings and smiles when Darcus lived here. Happier times before his 'friends forever' gradually disappeared, as Ardenne weaved her poison amongst them. Kenya had overheard conversations between Adosia and her son. He had rebuked her warnings of Ardenne's jealousy and mistrust, but in his heart Kenya thought he must have known his mother was right. As Ardenne's jealousy blossomed, it killed all laughter and love that entered their home.

Darcus' friendship group had been a reminder to Ardenne of how different she was from her husband, how loved he was by others. He was light to her growing darkness. Over time, her cantankerous nature and argumentative spirit picked fights where none was seen before. Kenya and her father would often squirm as Ardenne spewed bilious rants at their guests, more terrifying each time. It was not surprising when the barbecues stopped, and the Christmas cards failed to arrive. Those who swore they would be there in times of need never came back. Being alone in her tiny room was a constant reminder that she could not leave along with the others. Her room, her sanctuary, was also her barless prison.

Kenya knelt on her rug and held her 'room-mate'. Her constant companion was a small, dirty, pink stuffed toy squirrel with a missing eye. Squirrel had lost a lot of stuffing and his fluffy days were well and truly behind him, but he still had the magic to raise a smile from Kenya. Squirrel was an echo from the past, a loving gift from Darcus. Kenya had laughed at the ludicrous pink squirrel but loved him all the same. His cheerful expression throughout Ardenne's campaign of terror had been a comfort to Kenya. He lived underneath the floorboard for his own safety. Kenya knew that Ardenne would destroy him, like she had all her other possessions, if he were to be discovered. Squirrel did not hit, shout or make Kenya sad.

Dermott and Ardenne could learn a lot from Squirrel.

Chapter 3
The Last Time

'Kenya, Kenya!'

The sound of his voice made her smile. She ran down the stairs at speed and jumped into his arms.

'Dad, when did you get back? Did you see Gran-Gran? She phoned but Mum said I couldn't talk to her, and...'

Kenya stopped abruptly as her mother glided effortlessly into the room.

'So, look what the cat brought in,' smirked Ardenne. 'Darcus, I take it you still have a key. I would prefer it if you knocked.'

Ardenne stretched out her hand. Rings and bangles fought for space on her small, bony frame.

'The key!'

After a pause, Darcus dropped the key into her hand, as if to touch her would cause him to burn.

'I'm here to see Kenya. Kenya alone.'

Ardenne stared back at Darcus before marching out of the room, adding, 'Make sure I get my money by Monday.'

It was not until her footsteps on the stairs died down that Darcus cleared his voice to talk. 'Kenya, girl. You must look after yourself. Don't let her break you…'

'Why can't I come to live with you?' interrupted Kenya.

But Darcus continued over her pleas. 'It is more safe here than with me. There is no cause for the others to harm you here.'

Kenya sighed. She hated it when he spoke about 'the others'. It was that 'crazy talk' that stopped him from letting her live with him, as well as costing him his job in the city. Apparently, it was not good business practice to have financial advisors turning up late for work owing to having to fight 'the axis of evil' at the weekend. But all that aside, nothing and no one could stop Kenya loving her dad – whether people thought he was 'unstable' or not. She rested back in the armchair, preparing herself for one of her father's jumbled ramblings, but instead, Darcus thrusted a small fragment of a green and gold stone into her hand. It was warm, as if he had been holding on to it for dear life.

Slowly, Kenya released her grip on the fragment. The jagged inner region had part of an inscription on it which made no sense to Kenya. The markings were crude, as if made with a clay tool. A simple picture of a candle and fire surrounded by a triangular inlay of wood was above the markings. The triangle looked as if it had once been covered in an emerald-coloured stone. Darcus looked all around before whispering, 'Don't let anyone touch this. Guard it with your life. They will work out eventually that you have it…'

'What are you talking about?'

Darcus could obviously hear the concern etched in his daughter's voice.

'I am not in danger,' she continued.

'I know it sounds strange to you. It was like that for me at first, too. This fragment is one of many. They were once part of an ancient amulet. The Pangea amulet. The amulet is knowledgeable beyond human comprehension, and is an indescribable source of power.'

He pointed to the triangle made of wood imbedded into the fragment.

'These small pieces of wood are said to be from the tree of knowledge. These minuscule splinters have caused humans to fight, lie and die. This fragment and the others have the power to change the course of history, to control the earth.'

Darcus lowered his voice once more, looking deep into his daughter's eyes. She could not understand why the hairs at the back of her neck were standing on end. Even her breathing was more rapid, as if she had had a fright.

'Keep this fragment safe. It has the power to heal, but also to destroy. The world is more evil than you think. Keep yourself safe.'

Darcus broke off from explaining further as Dermott stormed in. 'Dis is not ya house now. I want you to remove ya self.'

It was obvious that Ardenne had put the witless man up to it, as he occasionally looked for reassurance or a nod of approval from his wife, who was standing behind him. That day Darcus did not feel like arguing, and left without looking round at Kenya.

Kenya woke up startled from her sleep. It was that recurring dream of the last time that she had seen her father. That was three years ago, the last time anyone had seen him.

The days after he had been reported missing were slow and painful. Each morning brought hope, only to exchange it for heartache come the evening. A heavy cloud descended on Adosia, who retreated into a silent world, where she heard all but said very little. Darcus left no message for his mother or for Kenya. No lengthy goodbye to right life's wrongs, no wise words to clear a pathway in her unknown future. No memories of a final embrace to comfort her in her loneliness. Just nothing. Since Darcus' body had never been recovered, it was the unknowing that brought the most pain.

At first, people clamoured to offer comforting words. However, when the days became weeks, their focus changed, moving on to the next news feed. The once-kind words became, 'Pull yourself together,' and, 'Your father would want you to move on now.' Then one day the words just stopped and the world carried on as normal, without Kenya.

Kenya's thoughts drew her to take the fragment from its safe place under the mattress. The fragment was highly decorated as if to hint of a past steeped in intrigue and wonder. The inner part of it was peppered with shards of the emerald stone which had once sat proudly in the centre. The worn, jagged sides of the piece showed that it had been held tightly for long periods of time, like a wanted prize.

Kenya carefully wrapped the fragment in an old tissue before placing it back under her mattress. Slowly, she clambered on to the creaking camp bed. Placing her head on her pillow, she pulled the thin patchwork blanket over her and cried quietly until dawn.

Chapter 4
Broken

She must have drifted to sleep because Dermott's screwed-up face was bent over her bed. Not a pleasing sight to awake to by any stretch of the imagination. Quickly, Kenya jumped out of bed, grabbing her clothes as Dermott unleashed a tirade of insults. Of course, she had purposely slept in, in order not to have to make his breakfast or iron his work uniform. To Kenya's surprise, he had blagged a managerial role in a nearby supermarket. However, it was not surprising that they were now desperate to rid themselves of him.

Kenya darted into the bathroom while Dermott continued his yapping outside the door like a Jack Russell that didn't know when to quit.

Kenya looked in the mirror. Her eyes were puffy from crying and her dry hair refused to lie flat. But it did not matter. She was seeing her grandmother today. Adosia's small frame and docile eyes sprang to mind. Her grandmother's hair was a mass of silver-grey plaits that were neatly tucked into a small bun low on her neck. Kenya often wondered where she had got her stubborn hair from. Adosia would spend many an evening combing through her granddaughter's hair; nimbly oiling her scalp and plaiting canerows at lightning speed. Kenya smiled. Soon she would feel the tenderness of Adosia's hands once more. It had been a long time coming. Kenya had not seen her since her father had disappeared. At the time Ardenne had been quick to add that Darcus was probably in trouble with the police, and that was why he had not got in touch with his own mother. 'Trouble makes trouble,' hissed Ardenne whenever Darcus' mother was mentioned. Not that she would say that to her face. If there was one person who put fear into 'Ardenne the fearless', it was Darcus' mother. Even the mention of her name made Ardenne and Dermott uneasy, as if she could hear their plotting. Because of this she was referred to by any insult going, with the prefix 'old' attached to it. Kenya was looking forward to seeing Ardenne squirm as much as to seeing her grandma.

'What sin are you brewing in there, gal,' yelled Dermott, thumping on the bathroom door. 'Get ya backside downstairs before I…'

The insult had slipped from Dermott's leaky brain.

'Before I… I… I have to tell you again!'

Kenya grinned. Stupid, dumb fool, she thought before opening the door. She was already halfway downstairs before he realised he was shouting to himself. Kenya's joy at confusing daft Dermott was short-lived as she ran into Ardenne. Before she could register the situation, Ardenne's fierce backhand sent Kenya crashing into the wall, knocking a mirror to the ground.

'See how your evil face buss up my mirror,' grinned Dermott.

'Don't just sit dere. Get ya backside moving and clear this up,' growled Ardenne.

'By the time you finish, the old witch will already be dead!' added Dermott, obviously pleased that he finally got to put Kenya down.

However, Ardenne ignored his put-down. 'Once you've finished Dermott's food, go back upstairs and put on something decent. I don't want to be seen on da bus with some gal tramp.'

Kenya picked herself up from the floor, catching a glimpse of her tired self in the broken shards of the hallway mirror. She looked unlike any other 13-year-old she knew. On those few occasions she made it into school, she would spend lunchtimes sitting alone, people-watching. Her peers became so accustomed to her disengagement that they soon became blind to the quiet girl in the corner. Kenya wandered from classroom to classroom, from one year to the next, without detection.

In the past, a student teacher had taken Kenya under her wing. Her friendly smile would seek Kenya out at break times and in the library after school. Under the teacher's guidance, Kenya made slow, fledgling inroads into being noticed by her peers. She began to see a point to school and looked forward to it; a haven from the hell of home. There were times Kenya came close to telling the teacher about her home life, but she was 'saved' by a bell or the need to catch her bus. At the end of the year, the student teacher left, along with concerns about Kenya's welfare. Everything quickly reverted to normal in the busyness of a new school year. Occasionally, a few teachers would mention Kenya as a 'cause for concern', flooding her with 'Are you OK?' conversations for a week until the focus moved on to a new initiative. She now thought that if a teacher spoke to her it must be because they had a managerial point or a grant to justify.

Lunchtimes were the worst part of the day. Different groups occupied their territories in the school canteen. They huddled around a vocal 'alpha' student. At times, the noise was deafening. However, in all the noise the silence surrounding Kenya was more ear-piercing. More painful. The chatter of students making plans to meet up, and the boisterous laughter tore through an envious Kenya. She cherished the thoughts of such freedom as she swept the hallway floor.

Chapter 5
The Boy

'Sister, there is no way you old enough to have a big daughter like that.'

Kenya's eyes rolled back into her head whilst Ardenne giggled like a schoolgirl as she collected her change from the bus driver. Kenya feared for her safety. If that driver could not see that Ardenne was clearly old enough to be his mother, then the chances of them reaching their destination intact was very slim.

There was only one space available on the lower deck and Ardenne made sure it had her name on it, even though there was an obviously pregnant woman boarding the bus with them. Her 'Christian' duties did not extend to giving up seats or any other charitable gestures.

As the big buildings whirled past the window, Kenya's mind filled with the excitement of seeing her grandmother. The only contact she had had with her was a birthday card three years ago. Kenya could always rely on Adosia to remember her birthday, and just knew the letter landing on the doormat was for her. She quickly opened the envelope to reveal a handmade card with a smiling black angel holding a flower. It read, 'To my little angel. Hold on to all that is precious. All my love, Gran-Gran Adosia.'

Kenya could still feel the warmth from those words before Ardenne had snatched the card from her grip that day. The more Kenya had pleaded, the higher Ardenne had held the card aloft. Keen to be involved in the new sport, Dermott had taken hold of the card, teasingly ripping small chunks out of it. Once the fun was over, it had been left to Kenya to tidy up the birthday card confetti. No doubt, Ardenne made sure that that was the last time her daughter received any correspondence from her grandmother.

These memories and more bubbled to the surface, causing Kenya's eyes to fill with tears. She watched the chattering children on the bus being fussed over by their mothers, eager to quieten their charges with bribes of sweets and cuddles. Kenya had no memory of her mother doing such things. Ardenne's coldness was so glacial that the displays of affection in front of Kenya were alien to her. She wondered whether Ardenne had ever held her so tenderly or wiped her sticky, sweet mouth and hands with such care. Deep thoughts evaporated as the bus came to a halt in the traffic along the high street.

Suddenly, she turned her head to the window, glimpsing a boy in the back seat of a gleaming silver Bentley. He was no older than herself, smartly dressed with a short, neat haircut. As their eyes met, something within Kenya made her bang her fists frantically against the window. Her heart and mind raced ahead, with every cell in her body wanting to claw through that window and join him. Kenya's ears were filled with the sounds of torturous screams which gained in volume until she fainted.

She felt her body rise and float like a bird carried to and fro on the thermal currents. In waves, a calmness descended upon her as she slowly opened her eyes. Kenya found herself standing on an expansive lawn. All around her the greenness stretched to the horizon, broken up only by a stone bridge leading to a large mansion house in the distance. Kenya looked down but was not surprised to see that she was now wearing a fine silk dress that caught the light as she moved.

A great lake appeared near the house, with three graceful swans leaving curved ripples on its waters. On seeing her, they turned towards her, calling softly and bobbing their heads in greeting. Suddenly, from the great house, Kenya heard a faint voice like that of her grandmother, Adosia. With her heart full of joy, Kenya sprinted over the bridge to the grand door and entered. The hallway was dimly lit and filled with a hazy mist, but again Kenya strangely did not feel any panic. Through the obscured view she could see a small, bright light ahead. The more she moved towards it the further away it seemed.

'Gran-Gran, I'm… I'm here.' For the first time, Kenya's nerves appeared.

'I know, child,' replied the voice so clearly, as if Adosia was standing a breath away. 'There are difficult times coming. I will need help, Kenya.' Her voice was tinged with sadness which touched the young girl.

'I'll help you, Gran-Gran! I will always help you.' Kenya stretched out her arms, desperate to find the source of the voice. 'Where are you?' Kenya continued to grapple with the dense air around her.

'The boy will help you once I've gone.'

Kenya heard her grandmother's voice, much weaker now, as if a thick fog had descended. As she yearned to hear clearly, the voice became more muffled. She felt the peace slip away as she called out to her grandmother.

'No, no. Gran-Gran, take me with you. Wait for me! Wait for me!' beseeched Kenya as the small bright light faded to nothing. Wildly, she ran blindly, searching for the voice.

'Gran-Gran! Don't leave me. I want to come with you!' Kenya screamed with her eyes tightly closed in fear.

Kenya could still hear screaming when she gained consciousness. To her surprise, she was leaning over her mother's seat with her forehead resting against the

41

window. The screams were now coming from an angry Ardenne. Her screwed-up face and the confused looks from the other passengers rained down on Kenya. As the traffic moved, the Bentley drove past with the boy banging furiously at the window too. Their eyes met and the panic she felt was also etched on his face.

'Behave ya self. Can't ya see everyone looking at you!' snorted Ardenne.

Embarrassed, Kenya pulled her fists from the window and sat back down. She could feel the intense glow of eyes trained on her as she hung her head low.

'Going on like ya na seen a buoy before!' muttered Ardenne to herself as she checked her flawless face in a compact mirror.

But I have not seen him before, pondered Kenya to herself.

Chapter 6
Reflection

Amit's mother continued her rhetoric on how she had sacrificed her life for her ungrateful son sitting beside her. It was only their driver, Milton, who had taken any notice of Amit banging hysterically on the car window at some strange girl on a bus. It was hardly surprising, he thought. He had often wondered why the boy had not gone off the rails sooner and run off like his father.

'Am I asking too much? I just want you to concentrate more on your violin practice. Reetamasi's boy can play Vivaldi's *Four Seasons* and he is five. Manubhai's daughter has been playing the piano since birth, and gave her first piano recital at nine months…'

'Mum,' interrupted a tired Amit, still staring out of the window, 'it was a toy piano.'

'You don't know the pressure I'm under,' continued his mother, fixing her sari blouse in the rear-view mirror as Milton attempted to reverse the Bentley into a bay at the local temple car park. 'These people are ready to laugh at me, to see me fall. Your father has caused me heartache and I will not allow you to…'

Amit's mother suddenly spotted a friend and quickly clambered out of the car to reveal her sparkling outfit. Darshna's insecurities temporarily melted away. The diamanté on her shocking pink and orange sari caught the sun's rays and many an envious eye was trained on her. Not even the stars could outshine Darshna in all her finery, and she knew that very well. Milton held her hand as she glided effortlessly over the carpeted pavement outside the temple. He had often thought she was a handsome woman with her mouth closed.

'*Kem cho*! Neelaben, how are you? You remember my boy, Amit.'

Amit squirmed as his mother placed her hands on his shoulders, thrusting him forward. Neelaben's obvious embarrassment at being spotted by Darshna almost matched his own.

'*Kem cho*, Darshna,' replied a nervous Neela. 'I can't stop long…'

'Sorry to hear that your daughter failed the entrance exam to Northgate. They are a very exclusive school. I was so surprised that my little Amit got into the even more prestigious boys' school, with a major scholarship. But don't you worry about your daughter! There is a perfectly adequate state school nearby. Actually, I think it's an academy now. They have a behavioural unit attached, so they'll take anyone. So, no pressure!'

Darshna gave a pent-up Neela a patronising pat on the back before swanning off with her elegant sari blowing in the breeze.

'I wish you wouldn't do that!' smarted Amit as he undid his shoelaces on the steps of the temple. As usual, Darshna was in her own world, giggling like a schoolgirl.

'Did you see her face? Not so smarty now! She was the first to make comments when your so-called father left. You just wait until they all hear my good news.'

'I was wondering why we were going to the temple midweek!' muttered Amit.

On entering the temple, the cool wooden floor under his feet and the ornate decorations immediately distracted Amit from his mother's constant rambling. In the relative calmness of the temple, Amit thought about his father, Pritesh. He had kept a hidden stash of old photos of his parents in his bedroom, away from his prying mother. The photos showed happier times in various far-flung locations. Pritesh's business was his world. Though he lacked the style and finesse Darshna craved, he had made up for it with an astute brain for making money. He had built up a considerable amount of wealth in the swimming pool construction trade to give his family a privileged lifestyle and high status. Darshna was proud that there was not a swimming pool on their gated estate that was not installed by his company.

With this localised 'boom' it had been rare for Pritesh to completely relax. Most of the time, his mind was a whirlwind of ideas and schemes to further increase his profits. In the early years of their marriage, Darshna had wished he would spend more time with her. However, she quickly realised that money and status could fill any void she felt in her life. That had all changed when Pritesh left. Shame was the greatest pain that engulfed Darshna. She swore whispers and stifled laughs followed her every move. Enraged, she had gone through the house like a dose of Epsom salts, purging all signs of her husband.

However, Amit could feel that there was more to this than a husband simply abandoning his family. Amit wondered if his father was being blackmailed or in trouble with the taxman. He often overheard his mother gossiping about her friends' husbands who were constantly away on holiday. What she failed to add was that the 'trip' was at Her Majesty's convenience. Perhaps that was the reason he had not been in touch? It was an ongoing mystery that Darshna blocked Amit from solving. The daily life of wages, bills and Darshna's personal allowance remained intact just as before. Each year, she received more than enough in dividends from Pritesh's various business adventures. All finances were dealt with by a trusted team of accountants behind the scenes. All Darshna did was spend without questioning. For Amit, it had been three long years since his father's disappearance. Time had not been a great healer.

'We are here to give thanks, you ungrateful boy.' Darshna disturbed her son's thoughts as she playfully ruffled his hair. 'And to make sure everyone hears about you getting into the exclusive Northgate Manor School!'

Darshna's last words were lost to Amit as he saw the face of the girl on the bus in a reflection on the polished oak wall panels. The panic he had felt in the car returned and he swiftly turned to greet her, colliding instead with a grumpy girl in an ill-fitting canary-yellow Punjabi suit.

'Oh, *kem cho*, Kapilaben! How are you? Have you heard about my boy, Amit?'

Darshna greeted the grumpy girl and her equally unhappy mother before immediately launching into her well-rehearsed routine of belittling her opponents. Amit's mind was elsewhere. Who was the girl on the bus?

Chapter 7
The Visit

The hospital was a hubbub of trolleys, nurses dashing
about, and beeping noises. Kenya thought it wasn't
surprising that people felt ill in hospital. With the peeling
white paint and the overpowering smell of disinfectant,
she had begun to feel queasy. Ardenne did not take note
of her daughter lagging several paces behind her. She was
a woman on a mission, striding off, pushing anyone out
of the way who dared to cross her path. At the end of the
long corridor was a set of stairs leading to Adosia's ward.
Without looking behind her, Ardenne flew up the stairs,
two steps at a time, with Kenya puffing behind her.
Kenya was eager to see her gran, but Ardenne was even
more eager.

'Remember,' growled Ardenne, finally acknowledging
Kenya, 'don't forget to mention the money. That witch
owes me… owes us.' Ardenne attempted to smile at
Kenya, who flinched at the unfamiliar sight. Ardenne was
only nice when she wanted something.

The swing doors flapped behind them as they entered the dimly lit ward. In contrast to the rest of the busy hospital, the sounds of Ardenne's court shoes and the occasional whimper from behind a curtain were the only sounds. A passing orderly directed Kenya and her mother to Adosia's bed.

Kenya took a sharp intake of breath on seeing her sleeping gran. She seemed much smaller, frailer than how she remembered her. By her bedside was a small cabinet with a few of her knick-knacks – a photo of Grandpa and Kenya's father, and a small passport picture of a young Kenya and her father squashed, laughing, in a photo booth. A photo you could not help but smile at – unless you were Ardenne. She tossed the photo to one side as she spotted the elderly woman's gold bracelet hidden under a magazine, and began examining it like a bargain hunter at an auction.

'Take your thievin' hands off my stuff,' bellowed the old woman, with one eye open and trained on the nervous-looking Ardenne. Giving Kenya a wink, Grandma Adosia's frailty evaporated as she waved Ardenne away.

'Go find a rock to crawl under. I have business to discuss with my angel.'

Ardenne opened her mouth to retaliate but the words dried up in Adosia's defiant gaze. Pausing for a second or two, Ardenne courageously sneered at Adosia in a battle of wills, only to disappear behind the partitioning curtains, muttering under her breath. In Adosia's presence, Ardenne was nervous. It was inexplicable. Somewhere deep within this grandmother was a great strength.

Kenya could not hold back any longer. A river of tears ran down her face. The more she tried to wipe them away, more tears ran down to join them. Adosia beckoned her closer for a hug. Kenya could not remember the last time she had felt the warmth of someone's arms around her and was almost reluctant to remove her face from her grandmother's grip.

'Hush, my angel. I don't have much time,' whispered Adosia, with her eye fixed on the curtain opening. 'We are living in evil times, my girl. Everywhere around us I see your father's words coming true…'

'Grandma,' interrupted Kenya, holding Adosia's hand tightly, 'Dad was sick. Please don't upset yourself…'

'Then we are both sick, too! Cause you see it, too. Death and destruction everywhere, but not by human hands. Flash floods, droughts, famine, power shortages…'

'You sound like Dad!' Kenya's voice had a frustrated edge. As far as she was concerned, her father could not face reality and had left her to fend for herself. How could he be so selfish?

'Your father loved you so much that he gave you his life – the very essence that protected you from his reality.'

The old woman looked at Kenya in a way that made her momentarily question whether Dermott was right in calling her a witch.

'A fragment of life itself, under your mattress.'

'How did you know?' blubbered a startled Kenya. 'Dad gave me that old fragment before... he left. He said it was to protect me but I never listened. He was always talking crazy. I just wanted him to talk "dad stuff", ask me about school, take me back with him, but all he was concerned with was saving the world from evil. I do miss him, but I guess I lost my dad years before he actually left.'

Adosia sat up sharply, leaning into Kenya.

'My angel, your father never left you.' She clapped her hand with a force. A blinding light appeared between her hands which grew as she slowly moved her hands apart. Kenya's mouth dropped open before she was drawn into the enveloping light.

Kenya opened her eyes tentatively. It felt like an age since she had closed them. She was now standing looking towards the opening in the curtain. Her pounding heart settled once she realised that nothing had changed. Must be having some kind of memory lapse or a funny turn, she thought. She had heard about these things from snatched titbits of conversations on those daytime TV programmes that occupied her mother's time. Kenya turned to apologise for blanking out, only to be confronted by herself smiling back at her.

Kenya stumbled backwards in shock, and was further startled as her grandmother helped her steady herself. Words failed Kenya as she looked at her 'other' grandmother staring blankly at her in her bed and the strong, vibrant one supporting her body under her foal-like feet.

'Those are our outer vessels, mere shadows of ourselves,' said Grandmother, nodding her head towards the other selves huddled in the far corner of the cubicle. 'This way we can talk in privacy.'

As Adosia passed through the curtain, a stumbling Kenya came face to face with a nosy Ardenne hanging around the opening. She seemed to be unaware as Kenya froze like a rabbit in headlights in front of her.

'She does not know you're there,' remarked the old woman, who mischievously blew in Ardenne's face, causing her to swat the air in search of the offending insect. Watching her mother battling with the air made Kenya giggle, but her attention was drawn back to the old woman's hands that were still emitting a somewhat duller light from her palms.

'Oh this,' remarked Adosia as if she read her granddaughter's mind. 'Both your father and you have the gift too!'

Kenya looked at her hands, both curled into a tense fist. Nervously, she released them, producing a white light which momentarily caught a confused Ardenne's eye. A concerned nurse persuaded Ardenne to rest in the visitors' lounge. She led her away, still swatting 'flies' and complaining about a blinding headache.

Adosia led Kenya down the corridor to where a big screen resided, repeating poorly acted community information to entertain the sick and injured in A and E. The waiting area was lit with bright fluorescent strips that exposed the yellowing paintwork and jaded posters on the walls. The din came from all around – tired children, bored of waiting, wailing in their parents' arms; drunkards challenging the receptionists to a fight; angry exchanges over the queues, and the screech of trolleys in desperate need of oiling. In all the mayhem, Adosia touched the large screen, causing the information to fade out. In its place appeared a younger Kenya, playing in the park with her father. Kenya touched the screen tentatively, half-hoping that her father would respond.

'Remember, these are mere shadows of a past time,' said Adosia gently. She stroked Kenya's hair softly to reassure her. The screen picture skipped to different memories, as if an unseen hand was controlling the remote.

'This is your moment.' Adosia touched the screen, pausing on Kenya's father handing her a gilded piece of broken pottery. Kenya half-smiled as she remembered her hidden disappointment. She had been hoping for a toy. This was the moment repeated a thousand times in her nightmares. The moment he walked away. In the frozen scene she could see for the first time the love etched deep in his face. This was for her. This was the picture she wanted to see in her dreams. She felt some of her long-held heartache disappear. He did love her; her mind was at rest. Kenya wanted to ask so much. Wanted to ask about the search for her father, but felt Adosia knew more but could not say.

'The amulet piece. Your father guarded this with his life. Now you must, too.'

On the screen, her father's piece clearly showed an ancient symbol for fire, showing its light-giving properties.

Adosia then produced another piece of the pottery from her pocket and placed it near the frozen screen, which was showing Kenya holding her piece aloft. The pieces fitted together like an old jigsaw. It was obvious other pieces were missing.

'Three, in fact,' answered the old woman before Kenya spoke. She looked on, shocked that her grandmother appeared to have read her mind, but Adosia's attention was elsewhere. The screen picture became smaller and smaller, till nothing remained but a small bright light in the centre. As the light expanded once more, an image of a highly decorated pendant came into focus. Its centre held a large emerald enclosed in gold. Kenya realised it must be the completed amulet – travelling through space. Kenya could barely recognise the symbols on the piece – air, light, water, earth, time. Before she could speak, the screen showed the complete amulet being pulled, tossed, fought over, as differing tribes grappled for control of it. As the various sides yelled and quarrelled, the amulet broke into pieces.

'It was deemed necessary to scatter the pieces throughout space and time to avoid the complete amulet falling into the hands of one,' continued Adosia. 'Absolute power…'

'… corrupts,' finished Kenya.

Her grandmother nodded in agreement. 'There are always points in history when the cowardice of many seeks to battle with the brave few. At this point in time, an evil, underground force is preparing war. That's where you come into it.'

Adosia turned quickly and walked down the corridor leading back to her room. Some commotion involving an impatient member of the public and several heavy-handed security staff sent people scurrying in the opposite direction. Still getting used to the idea that no one could see her, common decency told Kenya it was probably good manners to avoid people walking right through her. As people moved past Kenya and Adosia, they appeared to move in slow motion, only to revert to normal speed once they had passed.

A click of Adosia's fingers and Kenya was able to hear their inner thoughts and desires. The first couple of wants of 'cars', 'dream homes' and 'winning the lottery' were harmless, if a bit disconcerting. The odd thoughts were darker. An angry spirit hissed at Kenya as it passed, 'Give me the means… I would show them not to push me around.'

Kenya fearfully moved to get away from the venting spirit, only to be pressed to the wall by another screaming repeatedly, 'Give me the fragment!'

Calmly, Adosia turned, and a quick but deadly glare sent the spirit running back to its source.

'He knew about the amulet!' spluttered a still shaking Kenya. She tried to get a better look at the source, but the man and his internal self had already disappeared into the crowd heading towards the fracas in A and E.

'Oh, yes. Some will come in different forms to take what is yours to protect. They don't even know why,' said Adosia, pointing to the figure long gone. 'But it is your job to guard, to stay watchful.'

The two returned to the ward, talking of the days when the amulet was one. Kenya watched as her grandmother clambered back into the hospital bed. Back in her outer vessel, Adosia gave Kenya the jagged amulet piece she had shown her earlier.

'We are from a long line of light guardians. Used wisely, your powerful light will stop evil in its tracks. Your life is to guard your piece and hold on to this one,' added Adosia. She pointed to the other amulet piece.

The piece looked dull in comparison, and it was difficult for Kenya to recognise its water symbol of a body of oscillating waves merging into what appeared to be a large wave. As Kenya ran her fingers over the worn piece, the image immediately shifted to show a simple sand timer. The majority of the sand was still in the top half, trickling extremely finely into the almost empty container below. Realising she should be fearful of such apparitions, Kenya gave a delayed startled shudder and pushed out her hand to offer it back to her wryly smiling grandmother.

'This is for you to return to its guardian,' said the old woman, blocking Kenya's hand. 'There are guardians for each piece and this one is calling out for its protector.'

'Grandma, what about me? I am in need of protection!' spluttered Kenya. 'You want me to look after these… these things, to stop others getting them and find the owner of this one?'

'Roughly speaking, yes, darling.' Adosia tilted her heavy head to one side. 'I'm glad you understand now.'

Something within Kenya began to panic as the old lady became more frail-looking.

'How will I know who's the guardian?'

Frantically, Kenya tugged at her grandmother's hand. The piercing light from the old lady's palms was flickering as if she were subject to power failure.

'They'll know who you are and your light will guide you to them. The Children of Gabriel always recognise each other.' The old lady's eyes began to droop as she stumbled over her words, eager to be heard. 'Be watchful always, Kenya. Remember the prize you hold.'

Before Kenya could rattle off another tirade of questions, the light from Adosia's palms flickered for the last time. As the room returned to normal lighting, the sound of screeching trolleys, arguing patients and the rushing feet of nurses flooded Kenya's ears. Rooted to the plastic side chair, she remained motionless as nurses and doctors ran into the room, triggered by the sound of the old lady's heart monitor.

Chapter 8
That Girl

The noise and heat of the airport terminal was a distant
memory to Amit as he became 'one' with the cosy
massage chair in the hotel room spa, whilst his mother
was having a well-deserved (according to her) massage.
The sounds of the relaxation CD played backdrop to
Darshna's latest complaints.

'Every minute of my day has to be scheduled for
others. Constantly supporting charity functions and
coffee mornings. And do I get the recognition?'

She felt compelled to offload to the masseur. He was
eagerly pressing her mouth pressure points at this stage
in order to relax her, or at least turn her 'off', but to no
avail. Her use of rhetorical questions had reduced his
response to a faint, 'Yes, mam. No, mam.' Not that
Darshna was listening.

'I've worked so hard to get Amit into the top senior
school. No help from anyone. Had to find all those tutors

myself! Shreena's son didn't get in, and so she didn't invite me to her latest party. She is so bitter!'

Amit smirked as the unfortunate masseur's pressure point pressing became more akin to bashing a dud remote control. By now Darshna was halfway through a well-rehearsed rant on how she had single-handedly brought Amit up and how he had gravely disappointed her, and she could only hope he would prove worthy of all her hard work to get him into a good school.

At first, Amit had made a conscious effort to be as dissimilar to his father as possible. Every day without a word about his father's disappearance was hard. His concerns for Pritesh had slowly turned to anger at being left behind. It was then that Amit had made a conscious effort to be as different as possible to his father. The positive outcome he had hoped for was to finally gain approval from Darshna. He bought only the latest designer clothes, and all the related accessory trappings. Amit spent almost as much time preening himself in the morning as his mother did. Being the captain of his school's cricket first XI meant he was a slave to a strict fitness regime imposed by Darshna. Wheatgrass and alfalfa were firmly placed in his everyday vocabulary. Yet with all these differences, Darshna still could not refrain from comparing Amit to his absent father.

Sometimes, she would be conscious of the fact that she was unfairly berating her only child, but the anger within could not deter her. At times, she was akin to a spider struggling in a web of its own making. Amit recognised the tell-tale signs that this rant was going to progress quickly to 'one of those moments'. It was time to leave the hapless masseur to fend for himself.

A short passageway outside the spa led Amit onto the hotel's picture-card golden beach. He quickly kicked off his sandals and walked along the seashore, giggling happily to himself. He enjoyed the cool water gripping his toes as the waves lapped around him. The resort was full of 'A' class people – not the 'Tenerife lot', as his mother liked to remind him. Supermodels and footballers' wives were a-plenty, as well as 'old money'. The sounds of jet skis and tropical birds mingled with the sound bites from the other hotel guests.

'If he continues, I will sue him for every penny!' yelled a South African businessman into a mobile phone. He was red-faced with anger and sun as he paced furiously up and down his patch of this paradise. The more he shouted, the wilder his gesticulations became, as if it would aid his listener's understanding. As the hotel staff stifled their grins, his embarrassed daughter sat uncomfortably on a sun lounger waiting for her father's call to end and her holiday to begin.

As Amit passed by, he watched the unfolding drama of a suntanned mother yelling at her nanny. The children, bored with their mother's sunbathing, had taken to emptying the ice bucket for her wine down each other's swimsuits. The more the mother screamed, the more the children shrieked, leaving the exhausted nanny confused.

All this almost drowned out the gentle waves gathering around Amit, who had taken a seat amongst a group of rocks jutting out from the beach. The sunlight danced across the waves before they crashed against the rocks at the side of Amit's feet. Looking at the watery illuminations, Amit recalled the girl on the bus and pondered again who she was. She seemed to pop up in his thoughts with such frequency he no longer considered it odd that he felt he needed to find her.

Amit's attention was gripped by a group of small scuttling crabs that left tracks in the sand behind him as they rushed into the shallow pool at the foot of the rocks. A soft 'plop' announced their entry into their exclusive heated pool. As he watched the crabs jostling for prime position, he thought about the girl. Amit's hopes were dashed as he sadly concluded that it would be a hopeless task to find her. He did not even know her name.

His deep thoughts were suddenly interrupted by a high-pitched, '*Kem cho*, daarlin'!' He turned to spot his mother in her expensive swimsuit masked by her spa gown. A hotel staff member was following close behind Darshna, covering her with an ornate parasol, protecting her from the intense sun.

Her frantic waving meant one thing – she had achieved Nirvana, a place at the hotelier's top table. Without a word, Amit got up from his rock and trudged slowly through the sand towards Darshna, who was now waving wildly with his every heavy step. Something urged him to glance back.

The noise and chaos of beach life continued as before, apart from the crabs in the rock pool. Their shifting for position in their new home caused them to spell out 'KENYA', before a rogue wave came crashing into their pool.

Chapter 9
The Note

The healthy turnout for Adosia's funeral packed the front room and the kitchen. There was nothing like a well-catered funeral to bring out Ardenne's extended family. She was in her element. Ardenne had a captive audience who were subjected to her timely wail of 'Why? Why? Why?' whenever someone came to pay their respects.

'Pastor Brooke, sir,' quivered Ardenne, as a tall, dark man entered the room. 'Thank you for being here, sir.'

One glare from Ardenne sent the occupants of the comfy sofa fleeing in all directions as she ushered the important man to his prized seat. As Ardenne fussed around him, the slightly embarrassed clergyman did battle with the feisty ostrich feathers emanating from the crafty woman's hat.

'Sister Ardenne. Please,' interrupted Pastor Brooke, as a mountain of chicken wings, rice and peas were thrust into his face. 'How's the girl? I hear she was there when Sister Adosia left this mortal earth.'

'You mean when she "dead up", Pastor,' piped up Dermott, causing Ardenne to give him a sharp kick as he passed by.

'Don't worry 'bout her. Didn't even bother her. It's I who need your prayer, brother,' Ardenne sat closer to the worried pastor. Luckily, Kenya walked in and offered the clergyman a distraction. The room became hushed as she awkwardly stood in the middle of it, clutching an overladen tray. Her apron dwarfed the ill-fitting charity shop black suit underneath. The mourners were all in their finest and made her efforts look even more miserable. She now wished that the rug she was standing on would engulf her and put her out of her misery.

Pastor Brooke moved towards her to relieve her of the large plate of buns and cheese and Ardenne's tea in her personal cup. Kenya could feel all eyes on her. It felt like a lifetime before the room returned to its low-level mumbling, a mixture of plate scraping and chatter.

'How are you, Kenya?' asked Pastor Brooke. His voice was low and his eyes penetrated Kenya's soul. He had a gentle face, much younger than his years, which broke into a warming smile. 'You must be strong, little sister. Adosia wouldn't want…'

'Don't bodder the holy man. Can't you see him eatin' chicken wing?' interrupted Dermott. Kenya was ushered with speed out of the room, much to the protest of Pastor Brooke. Ardenne began wailing 'Why?' again, and fainted conveniently on the fluffy rug by the convection heater.

Kenya went to her room and sat on her rickety bed. A trickle of sunlight from a moth hole in her bed-sheet curtain entered the room, forming a mottled spotlight on the battered bedside cabinet. Drawn to the light, Kenya ruffled through her socks and vests drawer. At the back in an old pair of socks were the two amulet pieces. She quickly checked that no one was outside her room. The muffled noise from downstairs indicated that the sound system and DJ had turned up, and Ardenne's party was in full swing. No one would be looking for her for a while.

With this knowledge, Kenya scurried back to her bed. She placed the two amulet pieces in her lap. Her 'foster' piece still looked dull and sad to Kenya. A thought appeared in her brain as she stared at the pieces; she quickly dismissed it, tossing the pieces across the bed. After a pause, she tentatively looked at them again. Holding on to the fire piece tightly, she stared at it intensely. Just when she was thinking how ridiculous it all was, a bolt of light sprung from the amulet piece and bored a neat, small hole through the wall opposite the bed.

'Oh my…' Kenya mouthed, but her surprise moment was disturbed by a yelping Dermott outside the room. Kenya quickly hid the amulet pieces once more before emerging on the landing. Dermott had already gathered a small crowd. It was clear that something had burnt a precise pathway through Dermott's prized afro. Kenya could see that the light had not only made a small hole through her bedroom wall but had also made another through the wall on the other side of the landing. In the commotion, Pastor Brooke slipped Kenya a note; she quickly placed it in her apron, out of sight. It was not easy to slip anything unnoticed underneath the all-knowing nose of Ardenne, but they had managed to do so. Kenya turned to look at the pastor but he purposefully avoided her gaze.

'Nothing better to do, eh?' Dermott glared menacingly at Kenya. 'Y'betta stay put inna kitchen. Bad tings always 'appen with dis gal,' he added to the concerned onlookers who had gathered on the stairwell. Dermott's hair was still emitting a noticeable singed odour, which added to his annoyance. Unwilling to protest, Kenya trotted back down to the kitchen and began her duty of clearing the plates. She listened to the dulled thumping of music from the front room. She wondered if any of the guests would remember her name once the last piece of chicken had disappeared. Chicken had such a hold on her family that it was essential in all gatherings.

Though tired with work and her thoughts, it would have been futile for her to try to sleep. Once Adosia's wake had finished, Kenya was expected to serve during her parents' celebration bash.

'No time for dreams!' hissed Ardenne as she entered the kitchen. Her face was etched with a hearty smile that made Kenya feel uneasy. The impending reading of the will had put Ardenne in a good party mood. She had even laughed off the fact that Kenya had broken a mug whilst washing up earlier on in the day. How Kenya wished that she and not money had the power to make her mother smile all the time.

'Tomorrow I'll be able to buy d'world!' Dermott exclaimed as he marched into the room and proceeded to shove bottles of beer into an already packed fridge. Ardenne threw back her head with a belly laugh, and began singing her own version of Abba's 'Money, Money, Money'. Dermott joined her as she gyrated round the kitchen to her own music. Kenya was relieved when she was ordered to her room as the bottle-carrying revellers arrived. She could cope with her mother's lack of love, but enduring her singing was another matter.

Her mind began to work. The drawer... under the mattress... the amulet pieces needed a safer hiding place. She had a sudden idea. She speedily set to work, and when her job was done, she lay down on her creaking camp bed. The music seemed to float into the background as Kenya's eyelids became heavy with sleep. Her room began to appear smudged as she fought to stay awake. A sweet scent of lavender enticed her as she fully closed her weary lids. Her body became so relaxed that she felt the bed enveloping her further down, down into a deep sleep.

A pin-drop of a sound faintly awoke Kenya's senses. Still deeply in love with her bed, she chose not to stir. The lavender scent became stronger, willing her back into a deep sleep. A mild scratching noise and a muffled conversation made a curious Kenya gently raise one eyelid.

Shock ran through her body at lightning speed as she saw two dark figures scurrying around her room, effortlessly jumping from one piece of furniture to another. She shut her eyes once more, hoping it was all a trick of the light. Suddenly one of the creatures jumped onto her bed. Frightened, Kenya tentatively opened her eyes to see a pair of thorny hooves on her shins. The creature appeared to have the hind legs of a skeletal horse. His muscular upper body was short in contrast to the long, bony arms from which the knobbly fingers protruded. Crowning the terrifying body was a monstrous wolf head covered in sharp dagger-like bristles.

Kenya realised as they searched her room that the scratching noise came from the grey, calciferous talons of the creatures. Kenya's logical brain guided her to follow her instincts and remain rigidly still to avoid confrontation. The spotting of a sweet-smelling lavender pouch hanging from a hawthorn belt of the larger of the creatures gave Kenya a steely determination to remain awake at all costs. Periodically the creature would waft it in the air, deadening Kenya's awakening senses. One of the creatures was furtively sniffing around the apron hanging from a nail in the room. In her hazy mind, Kenya remembered the unread note from Pastor Brooke.

'She knows nothing,' the smaller creature announced, whipping books off Kenya's shelf with his protruding arms.

'No!' replied the larger creature. 'My nose never fails. I can smell something.' The creature's eyes swivelled in their sockets as it tried to tune in to the missing target. His bony hands glided over the apron, stopping abruptly over the pocket. He took one long sniff of the air as if to sample a fine wine. With every pant, he revealed his huge, ivory canines that hung low over his gaping jaw. Kenya controlled the urge to take a sharp breath. His claws hovered over the pocket entrance in anticipation. This is it, thought Kenya. The unread note could spell danger for her – if only she had read it straight away! Nervously, Kenya closed her eyes to what would shortly happen.

Unannounced as ever, a gruff Dermott opened the bedroom door, slamming it into the wall behind. The panicked creatures vanished through the bedroom walls before Dermott's brain could muster a visual cue.

'Ya mudder wants you clean up downstairs before she wake up tomorrow. Y'hear?' yelled Dermott. He was primed for a shouting match with the 'nuisance girl'. Kenya lifted her head above her blanket and nodded with a smile. A confused Dermott skulked off, slamming the door with as much gusto as he had opened it. Kenya had never been pleased to see Dermott before now. Only he could sabotage a demonic plot without noticing.

Feeling free from sedation, Kenya stumbled across the floor and collected the screwed-up note from her apron pocket. She held it tightly in her hand until she returned to her bed. Looking furtively to check all was clear, she read its message, written in her grandmother's handwriting: 'Beware, they know. They'll be coming for you tonight.' Kenya touched the words tentatively. Adosia's love was etched on to the note. She was still looking out for her 'angel'.

She carefully checked that Dermott was not on the landing before kneeling next to her camp bed. On the side of the mattress was a newly formed row of neat stitches. Carefully she unpicked her handiwork. Deep within the mattress was a bum bag where the amulet pieces resided safely in their new home. Kenya added the note to her prized possessions. Her thoughts mingled with her prayers as she sat slumped on her knees ur til she heard a voice from beyond.

'Gal, get ya backside down here!' screamed Dermott.

Chapter 10
Light

Darshna appeared to be in a dilemma, standing outside Amit's room. It was obvious that Amit was in the middle of some kind of nightmare, but she had a very important Kitty Club at her home.

The Kitty Club was a champagne and gossip group for the ladies of the exclusive suburb. Whilst the husbands pretended to enjoy a round of golf, their wives gathered to critique the ladies who had not attended that day. It was important to attend to add to the gossip in the hope that you would never be gossiped about. This was Darshna's turn to entertain the group. No expense was spared and the ladies were chatting merrily as the vintage champagne flowed.

To deal with Amit's 'little problem' would mean excusing herself from her own party – a tragedy worth avoiding. She remembered with glee that waking someone in the middle of a nightmare was detrimental to their health; or was that the advice for sleepwalking?

Confused, she pondered on this caring thought for a second before deciding that it was more important that *she* was fine. Amit would not want her to suffer on his behalf, she concluded. She swiftly gave the housekeeper strict instructions to leave Amit and not to disturb her whilst she entertained.

Amit had been chased for such a long time that he had forgotten how it had started. The loose branches from the heavily wooded forest conspired against him – whipping, scratching at him. His clothes were so ripped by thorns that they were only held on by the odd surviving buttons. Amit's body ached with the ongoing pace, but he knew the pain of stopping would be greater. The marauding pack were fast gaining ground on him. Their howling signalled their excitement of reaching their prey, as they jumped effortlessly from branch to uneven ground. Amit was not as sure-footed as he stumbled barefoot into the forest clearing. At least the harsh branches and thorns had given Amit protection; now his every movement was illuminated by the spotlight moon above.

Glancing behind, Amit noticed that half the pack had disappeared. His heart sank in the knowledge that he was running towards trouble. With the baying beasts behind him, there was no other viable option but to continue on his destructive course. Now the trees were so infrequent, he could see the other half of the pack bulldozing their way towards him. Amit was now so visible that to run or hide would be an exercise in futility. This was to be his end. Here, in a bare clearing without loved ones and final tributes. In frustration and fright, Amit lifted his weary head and let out a soul-rattling yell that reverberated through the clearing.

Kenya was jolted awake. She was drenched in cold sweat which caused her nightdress to stick uncomfortably to her back. Her heart was beating wildly as if she had run a marathon. Kenya could hear one of the amulet pieces vibrating at a low frequency.

Amit gingerly opened his eyes. He was lying on his bed. Relief slowly coursed through his still body. Just as he was reasonably concluding that the earlier event was a harmless nightmare, he saw a taloned dark creature raise itself from the side of the bed. Amit shuddered as he felt the beast's stagnant, hot breath on his cheek. Suddenly, another creature appeared, followed swiftly by another. In no time at all, the room was alive with dark creatures pawing, scraping and scratching any surface, including Amit's body.

From the corner of his eye, Amit noticed a large beast step forward, the stripes across his arms denoting his position of authority. He extended his fearsome talons so that they scratched the floor leading towards the bed. Without words he ran a sharpened talon slowly across the quivering boy's cheek. Fear rooted Amit in place as he resisted the urge to wipe the steady stream of blood running down his face.

Without warning, an opening appeared in the bedroom wall, through which two smaller armoured beasts hurtled out, breathing heavily from their run. As they surveyed the room, a further beast emerged from the shadows of the far corner.

At once all the other creatures bowed low and cried in unison, 'Hail, Hemlock, the supreme leader!'

Amit wondered how this great beast could have remained undetected, for he was at least half a metre taller than the one with the stripes, who Amit guessed was his deputy. He wanted to turn away, but his gaze was fixed on the leader's spine-like hairs that stood menacingly from his scalp. His expression was so terrifying that Amit fought hard not to take a sharp in-breath of air. The creature's very presence was as poisonous as his name. The newcomers bowed even lower, touching his hooves in reverence. Then the small beasts tentatively raised their heads, gauging the mood of their leader.

'My liege,' stuttered the braver of the two. 'We've returned from the Longley site. We searched the girl's room to no avail.'

'We could not stay longer,' whimpered the other tearfully. 'Her power is too strong!'

The simpering beast was interrupted with a sharp backhand to his head which sent him sprawling across the floor.

'Silence!' bellowed Hemlock. 'Shall I have to go myself?'

The other beasts bowed their heads, avoiding the fierce look of the leader.

'To trust such fools!' He pointed at the two huddled beasts quivering on the floor. 'I tell you, that girl is the key!'

An upright, smaller beast circled the bed. Though slender in stature, his dark presence enveloped the room. He possessed a smile that sent a chill through Amit's body.

'What should we do with this one?' The creature pulled at Amit's hair. 'I've bound him well for you, my liege.' He yanked on the thorn-like bonds that fastened Amit to the bed. 'For your... pleasure.' The creature grinned once more, which seemed to lull the leader into a calmer mood.

'He knows nothing! A useless little human,' growled Hemlock, moving towards Amit. He placed his frightening face a few centimetres from Amit's sweating brow.

'Do whatever you want, Darkclaw.' He smiled, sending a wave of shudders through Amit's weary body. 'Do whatever you want!'

Hemlock and his deputy left the bedroom through the portal in the wall, which sealed itself behind them. Immediately, the remaining dark creatures whooped and cheered, bouncing off the furniture and the walls. Darkclaw rubbed his reptilian claws together and leapt onto the bed. Amit made a futile attempt to pull at his bonds, which delighted the evil beast further.

'Be a good sport, now!' The beast raised his claws high above Amit's heart for the first strike. 'Keep still. I hate fast food,' he smirked.

Suddenly, the room was bathed in a blinding white light. The beasts' screams of joy turned into yells of despair as they scattered, running through the walls to freedom. The light continued to stream in, reflecting violently off every smooth surface. The toil of the torturous event caught up with Amit. As he wearily closed his eyes to the light, he was convinced he saw a girl's face. The mysterious girl from the bus.

'Kenya?' He continued to mumble her name until he fell unconscious.

Darshna was in mid-rant before Amit took any heed of her conversation. The red welts across his body showed that the previous night's terror had been no ordinary nightmare. The ugly scar running across her son's cheek did perturb Darshna on first sight, but she was in great need to tell Amit of the 'terrible wrong' made against her during the previous evening's revelry.

'Then after spending most of the night drinking my Cristal, she had the nerve to tell Divyaben what I told her in utmost secrecy!' Darshna slammed her slimming protein shake down. 'You are so lucky that you have me as your mother. That poor boy, Vikesh, hears nothing but the wagging tongue of Leenaben all day! And did you see what she had on? The woman has no shame.'

Darshna's diamanté-encrusted phone rang, filling the room with an old Bollywood tune.

'*Kem cho*, Leenaben. Lovely to hear from you,' answered Darshna in a fake, falsetto welcoming voice. 'I was just telling my Amit how gorgeous you looked yesterday…'

Amit pulled down his top and shuffled out of the room. He was about to trudge up the main stairs leading to his room when he spotted the mock Edwardian phone on its cabinet stand in the large hallway. He made an about turn, remembering the several phone directories in the cabinet stand's cupboard. An idea had formed in his head. He pulled out all the directories with great purpose, but lost hope halfway through his task when he remembered that he only knew the mysterious girl as 'Kenya'. No surname. Dejected, Amit slumped down onto the pile of directories and remained there until his confused driver found him. Milton, now convinced that Amit had finally lost the plot, picked up the young lad from his phone directory lair.

'Boy, your mother is going to go crazy when she sees all this mess!'

It was not until Amit felt the sharp pain running across his back that he realised that Milton was helping him to his feet. Immediately his dull eyes lit up.

'Milton! What's the number of the bus that leaves the centre to these parts?' There was such urgency in the boy's voice that Milton seemed taken aback.

'The H11 I think… No… It's the 182. It goes along the old high street to the hospital.'

Before the confused man could finish his sentence, Amit had left the house with his jacket flying behind him.

Chapter 11
Searching

Sensing that no good would ever come of anyone in that much of a hurry, Milton picked up the now-puffing Amit two roads away.

'I told your mother you were going into town,' said Milton, looking into his rear-view mirror at the exhausted wreck of a boy in the back seat of the Bentley.

Amit so wanted to tell him everything – the creatures, that girl, his mother's expectations. Instead, he quietly sobbed.

'I just need to find someone and then everything will be OK. Can't really explain. It's this girl.'

Milton nodded as if he knew what Amit's next line would be.

'I was young once, too. Sometimes you find a soulmate and will do anything to be with them.'

Amit realised that Milton was on the wrong track, but figured it was better than him thinking he was crazy.

'Mrs Milton, she was the love of my life. Followed her here from the old country.'

The automatic windscreen wipers went on as the first splutter of rain fell onto the car.

'Must have been love to follow her here to now freeze to death,' he muttered, turning the car heating up higher. He looked like he had other things on his mind before snapping out of it.

'So where to, young man?' he asked, full of renewed gusto.

The realisation of the enormity of Amit's task loomed in front of him.

'How do you find a girl you don't know, who is living at an address you don't know, to talk about a feeling you cannot explain?'

Milton caught Amit's deflated look in his mirror.

'Leave it to me. I know where all you young 'uns hang out!'

Kenya had been up since early morning, tidying the downstairs rooms. Even though she had collected numerous black bags of cans, bottles and crumpled paper plates, she felt she had made little progress, a feeling apparently shared by a foul-looking Ardenne. Lack of sleep and too much partying had made her more cantankerous than normal. Any sounds made by Kenya's attempts to clean up the beer can collection was met with a hate-filled dart of the eye and the kiss of the teeth. In contrast, Dermott danced into the kitchen with a look that said he had won the lottery.

'Daarlin', don't trouble ya self with foolish things!' He dared touch the shoulders of the very delicate Ardenne, who rudely shook him off. 'All things must come to pass,' he added, looking skywards in a pious moment. Kenya shook her head. Dermott occasionally came out with such sayings without actually knowing the meanings.

'Today you get de will, then paarty rum punch time!'

Dermott's spiritual moment failed to last as he fell about laughing wildly, dancing to the loud beat in his empty head. An uncontrollable anger rose within Kenya to the point that her brain buzzed loudly with the increased thudding of her heartbeat.

'Stupid, fool-fool woman! We gwan get the last laugh. When we spend up her 'eritance.'

Dermott cackled even louder at the sight of a visibly hurt Kenya. The more he laughed, the more anger bubbled up within the girl. His very presence was a nuisance requiring blotting out.

'What you look pon? Clean up, nah!' waved Dermott, ushering Kenya to get a move on. As Dermott continued to mock her, Kenya's head began to pound with ferocity. The room began to move in front of Kenya's eyes, whirling with increased velocity as Dermott pushed her towards the pile of black bags. The searing pain in Kenya was unbearable. She let out a scream from within her soul which filled the room. She felt her arms stretch out before her as if to reflect Dermot's abuse back towards him. Kenya's body shook with an incredible force which travelled down from her head and out through her hands with an even greater potency. Before Dermott could shout another insult, the kitchen was consumed in a blinding white light. It filled every corner and crevice until there were no colours to be seen. Just white. When Kenya came to, the clock on the wall was two hours ahead, with Dermott and Ardenne frozen to the spot.

Kenya hoped they were just playing around, but no amount of jumping in front of them, or prodding, could bring them from their silent world. It was then that she remembered Adosia had told her that her light would stop evil in its tracks.

Kenya stood staring at the last impressions on Dermott and Ardenne's faces – a mixture of shock and fear. Nervously she edged towards her mother's stony glare and touched her outstretched hand. Ardenne was poised to point an accusing finger at her daughter before she was stopped. Her skin was as supple as normal, in contrast to her statuesque posture. Kenya realised it was probably the closest she had been to her mother in years. She began to notice small details – how her mother's hands looked so pristine with their well-manicured talons, the strength in her broad shoulders, and how small freckles had gathered on her high cheekbones. Without a thought, Kenya balanced herself on her tiptoes and tentatively planted a small kiss on her mother's cheek.

The colossal divide between Kenya and her mother was so great. Had it always been that way? Kenya wracked her brain to find the faintest trace of happiness with her mother, but there was none to be found. She had sadly accepted that her life was not a saccharine-filled fairy tale. No happy ending. She paused for a while in deep thought before running upstairs to her room. She quickly grabbed the amulet pieces from their mattress hideout. A hurried 'goodbye' was given to Squirrel under the floorboard, before he was placed back in his hiding place. Kenya strapped the bum bag containing the amulet pieces securely to her waist before putting on her long coat.

There was a sense of urgency, for what she did not know, which propelled her out of the house and down the street to the bus stop at the end of the road. A long queue indicated that a bus was imminent. The usual suspects had gathered – the old lady with the enormous shopping trolley muttering about asylum seekers taking all the seats; a young mother with three small children hell-bent on escaping from the hold of her hand or from the double buggy she was struggling with; a tall, bespectacled young man in neat jeans and sporting a purple rucksack whose very appearance screamed, 'I'm an exchange student, please mug me!' and a trio of shifty-looking teenagers in oversized clothing who seemed likely to fulfil the exchange student's unspoken request.

The bus appeared, causing the orderly line to disintegrate as everyone tried to push onto the already crowded bus. The teenagers swiftly entered the bus via the exit doors and raced up the stairs to the top deck before the driver could notice. The old lady pulled a well-rehearsed karate move that doubled up people on both sides of her trolley, and she slipped onto the bus still muttering profusely. Kenya managed to squeeze herself onto the bus in the wake of the old lady's assault. Any jolt sent her into the young mum's buggy.

The journey took longer than normal, the bus winding its way to the town's main shopping parade. Kenya stared out of the grimy window as she thought about her frozen parents back home. The question of what to do next arose in her mind, only for her to draw a blank. She wondered what Adosia meant by calling her a Child of Gabriel. Looking down at her mismatched clothing she looked anything but 'angelic'.

Her growing frustration gave way to a vibration from the bum bag round her waist. As the bus passed along the main high street the vibration grew in intensity, emitting a sharp surge of heat that made Kenya yelp uncontrollably. Aware that the bored passengers were now fixated on her jiggling about, she rang the bell to indicate to the driver to pull in at the next stop. Disembarking quickly, she tried to notice her surroundings but the bustling nature of shoppers and businessfolk got in the way. Pushed this way and that, all she could register was the plethora of advertisement boards and shopfronts. Then the amulet pieces sent a wave of heat that stopped Kenya in her tracks. Turning her head, she saw a sign for the town's library.

Milton could see that Amit was feeling slightly uncomfortable by the driver's insistence that the top floor of the library was the place for a young boy to be seen. After shoving the hapless boy into an upward lift, Milton settled down on a comfy armchair near the newspapers and the oversized print books. He decided he would leave the boy to work things out of his system, whilst he worked out the winning horse of the 4.40 p.m. race at Doncaster tomorrow.

The lift doors opened to a different world for Amit. Rows of bookshelves were interspaced by pockets of study desks. Each desk offered privacy to the user, with high wooden screens on the sides and back, on which the teenagers who gathered there perched themselves. The librarians had long given up telling the youths to sit on the chairs, and had returned to the safety of the Expressive Arts section on the floor below.

Amit could feel the embarrassment rising within him. A group of girls suddenly interrupted their intense conversations to stare at him as he walked by, only to resume their chatting once he had passed. Boys from the local academy preened themselves in the shiny metal of the fire exit door further down, whilst the independent schoolboys acted 'too cool for school' by boisterously leaping around in the reference section.

Amit found an unoccupied desk and quickly set up home, taking out a small notebook from his jacket pocket, a pencil and his mobile phone. The only info he had to help him find this girl was the name 'Kenya', bus number 182 and the Longley site which one of the dark creatures had mentioned. He wrote all this down in the notebook, and pondered the impossible task in front of him.

A scraping of a chair indicated that a new occupant was next to him. Amit shuffled further into his cubbyhole and began googling the 182 bus route. He had seen the girl on that bus in the main high street so he had naturally concluded she must have started her journey before that. His mother was proud of the fact that she did not use public transport, and he could see why. The bus route seemed never-ending, taking massive detours just to get to the next street. Then, like a firebolt in his brain, he saw Longley Road bus stop. In his excitement, Amit pushed his chair backwards and found himself eye to eye with the person at the next study desk. He was confronted by an awkward-looking black girl of around his own age, with canerow plaits in her hair. They sat for what felt like a very long time, staring at each other.

A dry-mouthed Amit swallowed before speaking. 'Kenya?'

Kenya would have remained rooted to the spot if the annoying amulet pieces had not given her another pulsating reminder of their presence. This time she had had enough, and quickly placed the bum bag containing the pieces on the desk in front of her. Awkwardly aware that Amit was staring at her, she took her time before allowing her eyes to meet his again. Though his face had become a constant in her waking hours as well as in her dreams, Kenya noted the neatness of his labelled clothes in contrast to his weary, battle-scarred face. She looked down at her own mismatched clothes and wished she had chosen better that morning. She stuffed her feet back under the table to hide her odd, dirty white socks. Her brain was working overtime to find those all-important first words to say, to break the ice, make an impression.

Before she could filter her thoughts, the words tumbled out: 'You could have at least combed your hair!'

Embarrassed, Kenya returned to her cubbyhole and fervently began reading the graffiti on the desk as if they were prized prose. She was so angry with herself. Her nerves had got the better of her.

'Should we start over again?' came Amit's voice.

Kenya peered round the cubbyhole once more. A bemused-looking Amit was patting down his hair. She smiled, and the pair began talking excitedly. They were so engrossed in each other they failed to notice the slow exodus of teenagers leaving the top floor.

Amit roughly drew one of the dark creatures in his notebook. The very sight of the wolf-like creature made Kenya recoil.

'So you've seen them, too?' questioned Amit. Kenya's raised eyebrow and the tilt of her head was a reply that spoke volumes.

'Last night, I saw your face,' continued Amit. 'A bright light made them run before they could hurt me, and it came from you.'

Amit stared at Kenya, hoping that she would give an explanatory response, but she remained silent. Checking that the two were alone, Kenya slowly opened the bum bag. Carefully, she unwrapped her precious possessions. Amit took a sharp intake of breath as the water amulet piece emitted a low humming sound. As Kenya spoke about her father giving her the amulet piece, she began to cry. It seemed to Amit that the more she tried to stop, the more the tears flowed; perhaps thoughts that had been held within for years were being released, rushing out like a torrential flood.

Comforting his new friend, Amit gave Kenya a clean handkerchief from his jacket pocket. As their eyes met, he wondered if Kenya could tell from his gaze that he had his own absent father story to tell. Kenya leaned in as Amit recounted his own tale.

Amit's father, Pritesh, was a rotund man whose eating habits were in direct contrast to his wife's healthy lifestyle regime. It was the norm for Pritesh to conduct his business glued to his phone whilst munching on some deep-fried dead matter. Amit noticed that his thoughts about his father were not as halo-tinged as Kenya's were of her own father. 'He and mum argued a lot behind closed doors,' he admitted.

Kenya nodded. Amit could tell she understood. She clearly knew it was an adult pastime to yell in bedrooms.

'Then one morning he left with a suitcase, still on the phone. He just waved at me as he passed by in the hallway. Didn't look back...' He broke off and stared ahead. He was not used to talking about his father and wanted to stop the conversation. However, he could feel Kenya's eyes willing him to continue.

'It does not bother me,' he lied. 'I deal with things myself... or I ask Milton.'

Kenya quizzically put her head to the side, prompting Amit further.

'He's our driver,' he mumbled.

'Driver!' interrupted Kenya, playfully mocking Amit. He felt slightly embarrassed as she continued to giggle.

'Milton is more than that, really.' Amit shuffled uncomfortably on the seat. 'Especially since my dad left.'

'Maybe he didn't have a choice. Like my dad,' replied Kenya. He could see she wanted to believe it was true. 'Perhaps he went to fight one of those creatures,' she said, looking at Amit's sketch of the thorny beasts in front of her.

Ignoring her remark, Amit picked up the offending sketch.

'Why do they need these amulet pieces so badly?' he quizzed.

Kenya shrugged her shoulders. 'I only know what my grandmother said. These pieces fit together,' she added, placing the light and water fragments together. 'If they get all the other pieces then they have unquestionable power to do whatever they want. They seem to bring out the evil in some people.'

'Or good,' chipped in Amit. 'I don't want to think about what would have happened to me last night if you had not turned up with your light show!'

Kenya smiled shyly. 'I think this amulet piece belongs to you.' The water fragment let out a harmonious ring. 'I believe it is glad to see you!' She went on, 'We are the guardians. Just here to prevent the amulet pieces from falling into the wrong hands… or claws.'

Amit felt a wave of pride. He was one of the good guys, like a comic-book hero. He would be honourable, brave and fearless.

Unfortunately, the unexpected loud tannoy announcement of the library's closure broke the silence, scaring him witless. As he and Kenya laughed off their folly it dawned on him that the world order rested on the shoulders of two paranoid 13-year-olds in some London suburb.

Chapter 12
The View

The highest point of the town was a small shrub land called the View. From here the Wembley arch stood magnificently, and the rest of London looked to be within touching distance. This quiet jewel of a spot catered for dog owners and sightseeing pensioners. So it was not unusual to see a bedraggled old gentleman and his dog circling the walkway. And it was not unusual to see him stand and greet a motley crew of senior citizens who had slowly gathered around him. The few teens and younger dog owners who were also present quickly dispersed as if the very sight of the large aged gathering had unnerved them. The senior citizens continued to invade every spot of the shrub land until the last vehicle had left the makeshift car park next to the open land.

As dusk fell over the uneven pathways, those who were gathered hobbled and shuffled to a large yew tree. In front of the tree stood the old gentleman and his now menacing-looking dog. The throng gathering around him began to murmur and mumble until the whole crowd were baying and snapping at each other. A blood-curdling howl left the old man's body. The sound travelled around the shrub land, causing sparks of electricity as it made contact with the others gathered. The howl gave way to a chorus of wild sounds – of bones stretching, clothes ripping, and snorting. This continued until darkness fell and a clouded moon appeared. The shrub land was now occupied by the creatures that had plagued Kenya and Amit. They bounded wildly from shrub to shrub, emptying dog dirt bins and finishing abandoned cans of fizzy drinks.

Where the old man and his dog had stood was now tall, broad Hemlock with sharp spines covering his upper body. His lower hind legs were deer-like, but that was where the cute similarities stopped. The ripped muscles on his legs looked as if they were carved from the finest stone. It was only the pulsating veins running under his skin that revealed a life force. His hardened claws were still resting on the old man's comfy loafers. His scaly face was ashen, dominated by snarling reptilian eyes which surveyed the ensuing mayhem in from of him. His loyal terrier, now a robust dark creature, bounded up to him. The top of his thorny head was revealed as he bowed deeply in front of his leader, who acknowledged his presence with a nonchalant wave of his claws.

'Nightfall, my trusted deputy. What news do you bring?'

'My liege,' grunted Nightfall, 'your first earthly camp is secure. I've instructed the lessers to strengthen the fortress underneath.'

His claws pointed to a large group of smaller creatures burrowing furiously into the earth. Their towering overseer barked orders, whipping any lessers who foolishly dared to rest under the ferocious pace of the digging.

'Good. I've always wanted to go into real estate,' smirked Hemlock.

He looked sharply at his deputy to ensure he was acknowledging the witty remark.

'Yes, my liege, location is paramount.' The deputy bowed once more.

The two creatures silently surveyed the land in front of them. The shrub land gave a panoramic view of the town of Harrow below. The horizon was lit up by the amber hue of the street lights and the racing white lights of the miniature cars in the distance. Hemlock raised his clawed hands so it appeared that the town was cradled within them. The silence was punctuated with a hellish laugh as he enclosed the town within his claws.

'It is within your grasp, sire. We just need to locate the hidden pieces and…'

The deputy's sentence was cut short as the leader's talons enveloped his throat. It was common for him to experience Hemlock's quick change of mood. To swallow seemed impossible as his eyes met those of his leader.

'I want the girl. She knows where my amulet piece is. And maybe more pieces. She is displaying powers already because of your failure,' growled Hemlock angrily.

'My liege, whatever your wish I will…' stuttered Nightfall.

'You will find the girl alive and you will leave her dead.'

With that he swiftly marched towards the fortress construction, leaving Nightfall continuously bowing into the muddy earth.

Chapter 13
Helter-skelter

Milton had done the correct thing and phoned Darshna to let her know of Amit's whereabouts. Well, that was what he had thought. Darshna had more pressing matters on her mind and did not take it kindly that her 'only time to herself that day' had been rudely interrupted. Luckily, her Reiki man didn't mind her taking calls. Amit was to ask the maid to fix him his supper before she left for the night.

Darshna was an oxymoron that Milton had grown used to. How on earth she had produced a boy like Amit baffled him at times. Though he would never admit it, the old man knew that Amit was the closest thing to family for him. Although he spoke of Mrs Milton in the present, she had died years before Amit was born, reuniting with their only child, who had died in infancy. He planned to wait until Amit was settled at university before slipping off to build his dream home on his 'little land' back home. At times it proved difficult to follow that plan. He had lost count of the number of times he had packed his bags for good to leave Darshna's employment. It was the boy that kept him going.

In his mind, he parked Darshna's rants to one side and decided to give Amit and his little friend some time. Kenya's awkwardness and shyness immediately endeared her to Milton. Her lack of arrogance and self-worth was in contrast to the spoilt children he often came in contact with.

'So where do you live, little miss?' smiled Milton.

His kind eyes urged the shy Kenya to respond.

'She lives on Longley Road,' replied Amit, saving Kenya from talking.

'Should we give your parents a call? Let them know you're safe. Then we will drop you home.'

'Her parents are… out. They don't have a mobile phone and… er… em…' Amit's brain was clearly working overtime, to Kenya's amusement and Milton's annoyance.

'I think the lady can speak for herself!' Milton huffed. The old man paused to think. Surely, leaving her to go home alone was a greater crime than taking her back to her home? He could see that Kenya felt uncomfortable. He did not know that relying on others was a new experience that she feared above all else.

'I'm fine to take the bus home myself, Uncle,' Kenya smiled nervously. 'I've done it many times. I can call you when I'm home.'

Milton pondered as he removed his trilby, stroking his silver-white hair.

'I hear what you are saying, little miss, but… Mrs Milton would give me a right earful. I have to do the right thing, even if it's not the done thing.' He handed Kenya his battered mobile phone. 'Here, leave a message for your parents on the answer phone. Come, we will take you home.'

Milton guided Kenya and Amit to the library car park. As the pair dropped behind the old man, Milton could hear the unfamiliar sound of Amit's laughter.

It had not taken Milton long to find a parking space near Kenya's home. Worn down by Amit's lame excuses, Milton reluctantly remained in the car whilst Amit accompanied Kenya into her house.

On entering, Amit's eyes scoured the narrow, gloomy entrance. The brown and beige wallpaper made the already small hallway appear to be leaning in on its newest guest. The threadbare runner was covered with an equally worn plastic protective covering. He watched the back of Kenya's head as she happily marched on ahead to the kitchen, chirping about their time in the library. There were no staff to greet their arrival, no shrill voice of a mother to answer to. Just silence. The kitchen was a chaotic scene of clutter and pungent smells of rotting food which would have caused Amit's mother to faint. Darshna had taught Amit false politeness to a high level, but the words 'You have a nice place' got stuck in his throat.

'And here is my mum,' said Kenya, matter of factly, pointing to the stone-like Ardenne. Amit did not have time to register shock before Kenya added dryly, 'Oh, and this is the husband.'

Amit fired off a series of questions which were all met with a nonchalant 'I don't know' from Kenya.

'I am trying to understand! Why do you have to be so difficult?' moaned Amit, clearing a space in front of him at the kitchen table.

'I'm not being difficult! I just don't know,' retorted Kenya. She folded her arms defiantly, turning her back towards Amit. 'It all just happened!'

Kenya had no siblings and had thought many a time how pleasant it would be to have company. In that angry moment she concluded that being an only child was a blessing. She turned to see that Amit had moved on from the exchange of words to attempting to revive Ardenne and Dermott by prodding them with various kitchen utensils. When he graduated to using 'the element of surprise' – which consisted of launching himself at Ardenne in the hope of scaring her back to reality – Kenya knew it was time to divert her friend's attention. She found two plastic cups and the two enjoyed a drink of slightly flat lemonade on the slabs of DIY paving that made up the patio in the overgrown back garden. The long grass was a patchwork of rusting car parts and forgotten garden furniture. Dilapidated fencing gave a protective shade to the two friends perched on two upturned stone flowerpots. Silently they watched young squirrels chasing each other up and down the trees at the back of the garden, as if they were purposely entertaining their human audience.

Amit drank in the warmth of the pink-tinged sunset and the peace felt in this rundown garden. His eyes were closed, facing upwards towards the mackerel sky. Slowly the pair noted a faint musky, damp smell. It was not until a sweet lavender scent was detected that they broke from their trance to look to each other.

Before words could be uttered, a large beast was grappling with Amit, keen to relieve him of the amulet piece residing in his shirt's top pocket. Petrified, Amit stared into the steely eyes of his attacker. It was the commander, Nightfall, who had left his taloned mark on his face that awful night. He broke into a menacing smile as he began clawing and scratching. Amit's arms and legs kicked wildly in order to defend himself from the attack. Without thought, Kenya lunged at the beast, protecting Amit from the vicious onslaught. With a deadly precision Nightfall grabbed Kenya's arms, digging his talons deep into her flesh. For a brief moment her eyes met those of the commander. In that split second, Kenya saw the image of Adosia in the dark pool eyes of her attacker. She felt her grandmother was as close as she had been the last time they were together. Kenya felt strength returning to her weakened body. Channelling the searing pain, she swiftly turned out her palms, sending a pulsating bolt of light streaming into the eyes of the creature. Nightfall let out a guttural howl, as he flailed around in his blindness.

In shock, Kenya looked at her hands that had rescued Amit once more. She would have remained rooted to the spot if Amit had not pulled her to the relative safety of the muddy pond at the bottom of the garden.

'Look, Kenya! Look!' shouted Amit, staring at the murkiness of the abandoned pond. An ever-increasing whirl of light appeared within. The amulet pieces vibrated as the water rose from the pond, revealing a bright opening where once the bottom of the pond resided. Regaining his sight, the beast charged at the terrified children.

'Quick, jump!' yelled Kenya. She grabbed Amit's hand before he could protest and pulled him into the newly formed opening.

The young squirrels stopped their tree-bound foolishness to witness a large beast thrashing angrily about in the muddy pond below.

Kenya and Amit came hurtling down a large helter-skelter standing proudly above the other attractions on the packed pier. The tinny music from an old organ grinder played backdrop to the sounds of seagulls and chattering holidaymakers. Kenya looked blankly at a stunned Amit as they sat, legs tangled, on two threadbare mats at the foot of the helter-skelter. Even though she was beginning to become accustomed to the unimaginable, the speed at which they had moved from the garden pond to this unknown place left her baffled. The air was thick with seaside aromas – roasted chestnuts carried on the wind, vinegar-laden chips, and the sugary scent of doughnuts. Kenya straightened her crumpled skirt as best she could before helping a struggling Amit to his shaky feet.

It felt like an age before the two felt able to talk.

'There must be a reason why we are here,' said Kenya gently.

'Everything seems to point to a purpose,' nodded Amit, deep in thought.

Stepping from the cool shadows of the helter-skelter, the two sauntered along the cast iron-railed pier. The ornate lamps and bunting were home to a small group of opportunist seagulls that looked down at the pair. They were joined by gaping passers-by, their piercing eyes cutting through the surrounding saccharine-coated air. A concerned mother grabbed her pink-laced daughter as Amit brushed past her. The pursed lips and the sharp turn of her head spoke volumes. All eyes were on Amit and Kenya.

Quietly, as if not to draw more attention to themselves, Amit spoke from the side of his mouth.

'I don't think we are in Harrow any more!'

'I don't think we are anywhere,' replied Kenya, pointing to a newspaper stand in front of them. Rows upon rows of grainy black and white newspapers were fluttering in the sea breeze. All of them carried the same news – the coronation of Queen Elizabeth II. The red, white and blue pennants and bunting awashing the pier gave fresh meaning to Kenya. The neatly turned-out children, with girls in pretty dresses and boys with pressed shirts and shorts, looked so alien to Amit. Highly coiffured women in fitted pastel dresses held on to their matching handbags whilst the trilby-wearing men puffed clouds of cigarette smoke in their rolled-up shirt sleeves and braces.

A gruff voice shocked Kenya and Amit back to the new reality.

'Oi! What are you standing around for? Get a move on before I call the coppers on yah!' He signalled to a policeman standing in the distance, which encouraged Kenya and Amit to move on quickly to the pier entrance.

'I think we are the main attraction on the pier!' exclaimed Amit, looking over his shoulders to check the policeman was off their trail. 'Where are we?' he added.

'We've gone back in time – 1953, to be precise.'

'1953! That's ancient,' shrieked Amit. 'What's brought us here?'

'The amulet pieces,' smiled Kenya. The sunlight had broken through a cloud and was settling on her face. Considering they were confronted with the unknown,

Amit thought Kenya had never looked as much at peace, or as confident as now. He would have happily stood for hours staring at Kenya if it had not been for the low hum emitting from his amulet piece.

'No time to lose!' shouted Kenya as she sped down the stone steps towards the pebble beach below. Amit followed behind as the quiet hum of the amulet pieces increased in pitch as they changed their direction across the beach.

'The pieces are leading us somewhere. The higher the pitch, the closer our destination,' puffed Amit, finally catching up with Kenya.

'Our destination could be another amulet piece,' exclaimed Kenya excitedly.

'Or danger,' added Amit. His response was met with such a look of disdain that he decided it would be wise to keep negative thoughts to himself in future.

They followed the chimes to a quieter part of the beach, away from the gawping crowds of day trippers. The amulet pieces sonorously marked the spot and the pair began to dig. At first the scrapings were a gentle movement of pebbles that grew into a frantic excavation buoyed by Kenya's enthusiasm.

'There is a piece here. It's definitely here!' assured Kenya.

The children lifted huge clumps of stone and debris until the spot was marked by a deep hole at least as deep as they were tall. Exhausted, Amit fell to his knees.

'Definitely here!' he mocked, staring at the waste of his energy before him.

He picked up a clump of earth and stone, hurling it into the sodden side of the freshly dug pit. Before he could continue with his angry outpouring, a delicate chime reverberated.

'Definitely here!' repeated Kenya, with an edge to her voice that could cut steel. Her eyes met a sheepish-looking Amit, less defiant, and eager to deflect attention towards the chimes emitting from the hole. The sound continued to rise above the two like a cloud of cathedral bells raining down on them. Excitement bubbled up inside Amit as he gently removed debris from one side of the pit. The chiming symphony reached its climax as a shard of sunlight hit a dirt-covered object embedded in the collapsing wall.

'If I hold on to you…' began Kenya.

'… I will reach it,' finished Amit.

The object began to sing of its presence so loudly that Kenya looked furtively towards the pier. Surely someone would hear the noise? The inquisitive looks from holidaymakers never came. Not a single eye met Kenya's.

'Nearly there,' grimaced Amit. He tugged at the object until it was free from the earth and pebbles. Kneeling, he held the prize in his grubby hands and began to rub years of dirt from the surface. All their digging was for an irregular-shaped shard of pottery and metal. Another break in the cloud allowed the hazy sunlight to pick up the less worn areas of the piece. A faint marking could be seen, which caused a flutter within Kenya.

'Can you read it?' asked Kenya.

'Not yet,' replied Amit. He continued to rub at the surface of the disc, which emitted a satisfied low hum. Kenya took a deep intake of breath as Amit revealed a delicately decorated picture of the earth surrounded by five pairs of hands, which shifted to reveal a sand timer.

'I saw the sand timer when my grandmother gave me your amulet piece,' smiled Kenya. It felt like such a long time since that moment. 'The piece needs its owner,' she continued, touching the ever-shifting pictures.

'Just like my piece did,' grinned Amit, placing his hand deep into his pocket to bring out his share of the amulet.

Kneeling into the pebbles and earth on the mound, the two excitedly fitted the three amulet pieces together. Before they could ask each other, 'What next?' a deep hum rose from the pieces, whooshing straight into the clouds before descending in a cacophony of bells. The ground began to shake violently, sending waves crashing against the underbelly of the pier. Kenya grabbed the amulet pieces, shoving them firmly back into her bum bag.

'Hold on!' yelled Amit, as wave upon wave twisted the pair high into the sky above the pier.

Chapter 14
Nightfall

Hemlock's howl filled every corner of the underworld camp. When Nightfall entered the hollowed space reserved for him, he was greeted by the hapless body of a young guard. No feelings of remorse or sadness filled his hard heart as he roughly kicked the bloodied hind legs of the unlucky one in order to pass. He should have known to leave the supreme leader at the first sign of his rage, thought Nightfall. His terrible temper was well known since his cub days. Nightfall had risen to his position by unquestioningly following orders and being watchful of his supreme leader's deadly claws.

Hemlock snarled and growled, pacing the torch-lit room. His commanders and oracles knew best not to attempt to pacify him. Maps and potion bottles were strewn across a roughly made table. What was left of the chairs were embedded deep into the muddy walls.

'How could you be so stupid? I can feel their power growing daily. Someone is helping them!'

Hemlock's voice was like thunder, travelling through the very ground he stood on.

'Sire,' began Nightfall, 'there is a field of some kind surrounding her that my best generals cannot…'

'No feeble excuses!' barked Hemlock. 'Remember your place, General. You can be easily replaced!' He gave a sinister, sly glance at the crumpled body of the young guard. 'Easily replaced!' he repeated, menacingly. He slowly walked towards the Command Hut entrance, trampling heavily on the former guard strewn on the floor like a cheap rug. Nightfall bowed low until the supreme leader's bark was a mere whisper deep within the compound.

The hut was a chaotic scene, with the high table acting as the epicentre. Dutifully, Nightfall began clearing the piles of documents and old parchment that were scattered under the table. His thoughts drifted to 'that girl'. He had met many human leaders in his time. He had seen the rise of Rome and howled on the hillsides looking down on Babylon. Though humans were innately stupid, he could see the 'wolf' within many of their greatest leaders. Many a beast would dismiss human achievements by sniffily remarking that the individual was obviously a wolf hybrid in heritage. However, this unassuming girl was causing havoc amongst his squad, and as a result the supreme leader's mood was darker than usual.

As he placed the fiercely torn papers on the desk, he tried in earnest not to read, but curiosity won. With an eye nervously trained on the opening to the hut, he gazed down on the works. Much was written in the old wolfish tongue and he cursed himself for not having paid more attention to his studies as a cub. It spoke of a time when the earth was so young that the ground was still hot underfoot. Both angels and humans lived and worked together. The animals roamed free, following their natural law undisturbed and safe from sapiens' meddling. Any disputes were quickly resolved, as harmony was the natural equilibrium point. The powerful amulet of old was shared amongst all. It gave guidance when needed and was a well of energy to keep the earth warm and fruitful.

Such was the peace amongst the earth-dwellers that intermarriage of heavenly and earthly beings became common. Their offspring ran faster, grew stronger and thought smarter. These super-beings formed two distinctive camps. Some shared the appearance of humans, such as the skyscraping giants. They were known as the Angel Sapiens. The others shared more characteristics with the other animals, such as the minotaurs of the classic stories. These more fauna angels formed the clan called the Nephanaks. It was not long before the admiration and praise amongst these super beings swiftly turned into whispers, backbiting and jealousy. Families were pitched against each other in a show of super-being strength. Access to the amulet was key, as it gave advantage to those who had it – the first taste for many of the delights of power.

Sensing a chance to further open a widening chasm, the humans took sides. They switched allegiance in line with the see-sawing balance of power between the Angel Sapiens and the Nephanaks. Great families spoke of taking the amulet for themselves, and wars were fought to gain advantage. Nightfall recognised his own amongst the Nephanak family names.

As the battles raged on, a small band of Angel Sapiens guarding the amulet received repeated visions to leave their lands and set themselves apart. It was decreed by these five elders to scatter pieces of the great amulet throughout eternity to avoid the destruction of the earth by one crazed group or another. This angered the Nephanaks greatly. What right did the Angel Sapiens have to decide this? Who gave them the authority to do such a thing?

As the mistrust continued, the earth became a two-tier society. The Angel Sapiens grew in the light of the day, creating laws and borders. In contrast, the Nephanaks skulked around in the hedgerows at dusk, ever distrustful of the light. They spoke of lost privileges and broken promises, till their hearts shrank and darkened. The spiky thorns of hatred coursed through their veins, piercing their very skin to create a coarse carpet of fur on their broad backs. The battle scars of years of clashes had left them with an undulating, impregnable breastplate. Wide, reptilian legs stood like scorched tree trunks, rooted in the evil land they now possessed.

The Angel Sapiens danced and sang merrily with the mortals until only a small band of talent-holding descendants remained. In contrast, fear had kept the now dark-dwellers united against the mortal merrymakers. Their clans fought and married, producing offspring more powerful and hate-filled than their ancestors. Thus, war and bitterness was etched into centuries of their history. The wolf hybrids known as Lycans adapted to the dark, murky world underground. They were sharp in thought and quickly harnessed the power to shapeshift into other beings at will. The sly, power-hungry Lycans scrapped their way to the top of the pile to become the supreme leaders of the Underworld. They revelled as their dark talents increased, whilst the Angel Sapiens dwindled into folklore. Above the ground, no one spoke of the Angel Sapiens of old, or of the amulet pieces.

The text continued with long successions of supreme leaders and those in the future who would harass 'the people of the light'. All through the centuries, dark-dwellers had surreptitiously tipped the balance in their favour. Wild parties were held underground as the children of men slaughtered each other in wars caused by the Nephanaks' covert meddling. The underground merriment that followed could only be drowned out by the tanks and mortar shelling of the cities above ground. The tales of the carnage humans inflicted on each other was celebrated with such gusto in the text that Nightfall puffed out his proud chest in approval. These were the tales that had been taught to him during his early training. Here Nightfall learnt obedience to follow instructions and give reverence to his superiors. Slowly, the haunting doubts he had harboured of not being a true Lycan had been tamed.

He eagerly pored over the documents for more glimmers of evil deeds committed by his forefathers. The burgeoning pride within him was instantly deflated – the Oracle vision of the future came into focus. He yearned to see the future with the famed amulet pieces reconnected in the hands of the Nephanaks. But, no! Page after page he turned with anger and disbelief. With rage he curled his fists so tightly that his talons left deep welts on his scaly palms. A red mist descended on him until he was unable to view the text. It was that girl! How could the name of a mere mortal who had no power or position amongst her own kind be written here? Here, amongst the great names of old! The fire within his belly grew until it consumed the torn, arranged pieces of text on the table with a firebolt. All that remained were faint scorch marks where once the text had lain.

Nightfall stormed from the back entrance of the hut, hitting out at any subordinate who got in his way. Subconsciously, he locked what he had read and seen in his once-proud chest. A seed had been sown, causing a fine-line crack to appear in his shrivelled, obsidian heart.

Chapter 15

Return

She had felt it a mere second since she last opened her eyes, but her senses had convinced her wrongly. Kenya stared up into a star-filled sky. The names of constellations came to mind, and the stories associated with them. She felt calm, staring in wonder at each purposefully placed light; she felt at peace. No worries about the future or the past. Just a restful peace in the presence that slipped away as quickly as it had arrived when a groggy-looking Amit came into vision. He was clutching his dishevelled head. His attempt to clear his foggy senses by wildly shaking his head made him feel worse. Kenya suspected the corner of one of the patio slabs was the main culprit responsible for his discomfort. She smiled.

'Longley Road,' whispered Kenya. The sight of the overgrown garden brought temporary relief until she attempted to sit up. The sleeves of her flimsy coat were jaggedly torn to reveal deep talon marks. Searing pain filled her body, giving her no choice but to cry out.

'Kenya! Kenya, are you alright?'

In the half-light from the neighbouring house, Kenya could see the concern etched on Amit's face. She decided for his sake she would have to internalise the pain somehow, in order not to alarm him again.

'I need to get you in to the house quickly,' urged Amit. Kenya could hear a slight panic in his voice. He gently cradled her onto her unsteady feet, and they took slow shuffles through the back door of Ardenne's house, into the kitchen. Kenya welcomed the chair underneath her while Amit rushed around the kitchen, flinging open cupboards in a frantic search for treatment for Kenya's wounds.

'This should do the trick!' announced Amit confidently. Amassed on the kitchen table was an array of old antiseptic products, plasters and threadbare bandages. As he administered the wares, Kenya silently noted that it was his caring attention that gave her the most pain relief. It was not long before a smile returned to her lips.

'There's no food in this place!' moaned Amit, with his head buried in the fridge. Ardenne's love of takeaways meant the barely cold fridge was a haven for condiments way past their sell-by date, and Dermott's lethal home-brew concoctions. 'You'll have to come back to my house!'

Amit spoke with such authority that Kenya was taken aback.

'It will be too dangerous for you to remain here,' he added. His voice had returned to its normal level as he shut the remaining cupboard doors.

'The company will do you good,' he remarked, nodding at the mannequin, Ardenne, in their midst. As soon as Amit erupted into laughter at his own joke, he seemed to suddenly panic. He dashed along the hallway leading to the front door with a hobbling Kenya in his wake.

'Will you just calm down?' laughed Kenya, shaking her head. She considered the bump on his head may have been more serious than she first thought.

'We left Milton in the car all this time,' protested Amit.

'He can't possibly be outside still,' chortled Kenya. 'We've been away for hours!'

Her laughing protests were silenced as the two peered through the broken slats of the hallway blinds. The nearby street light illuminated the distinctive silver Bentley with the familiar outline of a sleeping Milton in the driver seat. His head was tilted back, with his favourite trilby perched precariously on his forehead. For a second Kenya thought she saw an image of her grandmother in the car's rear window, but her heart sank after the next blink of her eyes. No doubt a cruel trick of the light, coupled with her deepest want.

Amit felt brave, stepping first out of the house towards the car. This was his time to show Kenya how courageous he could be. He would test the way to make sure no demonic creatures were in the vicinity. He glanced back towards Kenya for reassurance before tapping gently on the front window of the Bentley. A sudden awakening snort from Milton made Amit jump, startling the driver in response.

'What, what time... why... Get in the car, boy! This instant!' spluttered a confused Milton. Turning off the remaining lights, Kenya locked the door behind her before slowly sliding into the back seat to join Amit and Milton in mid-conversation.

'Your mother is going to kill me – and you!' bellowed Milton. He was in full tirade mode and Amit's previous interjections had failed to deter him. 'Nine o'clock! Nine o'clock!'

'You looked happy asleep. We didn't think it right to wake you. You work hard and you obviously don't get much downtime. You just needed to rest,' soothed Kenya.

Milton's anger dissipated as he nervously flattened his jacket lapels and neatened the now comical trilby perched high on his head.

''Tis true. His mother works me hard. Drive here. Drive there...'

'No wonder you fell asleep,' interrupted Amit. Sensing that Kenya had worked her charm, he added, 'You work too hard!' before patting Milton gently on the shoulder.

'Too true, too true,' agreed Milton, forehead creased in deep thought before he snapped back into reality. 'What about your mother?' he asked Kenya.

'Work. Night shift. She will be home late,' Amit quickly replied. He hated lying to Milton but the truth had become so difficult to explain.

'She's got stuck somewhere,' added Kenya, and Amit smiled, thinking about her mother rooted to the kitchen floor.

'I didn't think it was right to leave Kenya in the house on her own.' Amit looked into the eyes of the old driver. 'We can't leave her.'

Without a word of protest, Milton did the right thing and listened to his heart.

Chapter 16
Flood

The day's events had made Kenya weary, and she drifted into a heavy sleep. It was the sudden jolt to the car that awoke her. It was the tell-tale signs of the numerous traffic-calming bumps that signalled their entry into the private gated estate where Amit and his mother, Darshna, resided.

Rows upon rows of palatial homes were interspersed with mansions in various stages of being built. It had become fashionable to buy a property worth millions in order to raze it to the ground to build a larger mansion. This was a signal to others that greater wealth than themselves was moving into the area. Competition was keen and therefore became the most cumbersome chain that hung around Darshna's slender neck.

The unnervingly quiet estate changed in an instant as Milton turned the handle of the one of many folding patio doors at the back of the house. The conservatory led to the vacuous, open-plan kitchen entertaining area. The three latecomers were stopped in their tracks by a milieu of thundering, pulsating bhangra music and the chattering noise of partying guests. Black-suited staff with heavily laden silver trays held high in the air manoeuvred through the throng. Suddenly, the bejewelled frame of Darshna came into view, in mid-conversation as if Amit had been present at her side all evening. If Darshna was concerned with the suspected disappearance of her son and driver, she was keeping it well hidden.

'... and you must meet Raj Uncle and his entrepreneurial son, Dipak. He plays golf with the Head of St Augustine...'

She halted her conversation as her brain finally caught up with the spectacle in front of her. Her smiling face quickly grimaced, only falsely reverting back when her guests passed near her.

'How could you come downstairs looking like dat!' She spoke through clenched teeth, conscious that the eyes of society's finest may be fixed on her. 'This is my one chance and you are purposefully trying to ruin my life...' Darshna stopped her rant to take stock of Kenya. 'And why are you standing there?' Before Kenya or Amit could reply, Darshna had already begun pushing the pair out of the way of prying eyes.

Milton was far too jaded for Darshna's shrieking and saw this as a good a time as any to slip away.

'You, upstairs – shower, change, come downstairs and entertain,' she snapped at Amit at the foot of the main staircase. 'You, in the staff kitchen,' she bellowed at a shocked Kenya. 'And get the uniform on. Standing around acting like you are a guest! Don't expect me to pay your wages in full!'

Amit shrugged his shoulders at Kenya, who decided it was safer to play along with Darshna's version of events. She gave her 'new boss' an awkward curtsey and followed Amit towards the kitchen entrance near the main stairwell. Fortunately, the chimes of the doorbell gave Kenya and Amit time to sneak upstairs as Darshna fluttered to the attention of her new party guests.

As soon as Amit's bedroom door shut behind them, the two children stared at each other in disbelief.

'Is that what normally happens when you introduce a friend to your mother?' giggled Kenya, making herself comfortable on a large furry bean bag.

'Count yourself lucky,' Amit replied loftily. 'She did give you a job!'

Kenya felt that response deserved a lush pillow to be firmly thrown at Amit's head. The ensuing pillow fight would have continued had it not been for the unwanted interruption of the low hum emitted from the amulet pieces. Without the need to speak to each other, they sadly knew that this was no time for childish pursuits.

Amit checked that all three amulet pieces were safe in Kenya's bum bag before following his mother's advice to shower.

As she waited for Amit's return, Kenya had a nosy look around his room. Neatly framed certificates of achievement were displayed on his wall, alongside a state-of-the-art computer gaming system. The two computer screens dwarfed the wall they were mounted on. Three unsteady piles of revision guides, Bond papers and notes clothed his work desk, with a heavily graffitied exam timetable anchored to a sorry-looking cactus plant by a limp spine.

Kenya thought of her own draughty bedroom which would have easily fitted into one of the wardrobes that dominated the room. Her thoughts paused with the sound of Amit's return. His chatter was lighter, as if worries were washed away in the shower, too. His wet feet left small damp patches as he searched for matching socks. At first, Kenya did not believe her tired eyes. Small, translucent flashes of light fell gently from his bare feet and arms as he scurried around the room. As his useless chatter progressed, Kenya saw fine, silver scales appearing on his limbs. The scales caught the light like cut diamonds, scattering a mottled shimmer onto all the flat surfaces in the room. Before Kenya could speak, Amit had already began to stare at his arms in disbelief.

'It's the water amulet!' shrieked Kenya excitedly. Amit's amulet piece hummed a higher frequency from the bum bag. The iridescent light display emitting from the scales accompanied the new sounds in unison.

'You have the light, and this is my skill?' questioned Amit, his face a tad disappointed.

'You must practise!' responded Kenya, ignoring the self-pity in his voice. 'Concentrate. Think waves, water… Just think!'

Amit closed his eyes and thought waves, streams of water, monsoons… and then he focused on his father. The more he tried to shake the thoughts away, they came back in abundance. He remembered being carried aloft as a small boy, his father's hearty laugh and his smile. At first it was a tingling sensation, until he felt his whole ribcage shake as it battled to hold back a flood of emotion. The fear of letting go subsided as he heard the rush of water in his brain. At first there was nothing but a trickle of water emitting from the centre of one palm. Before Amit could make a sarcastic comment about his lacklustre talent, a torrent of water washed through the room. The jets of water streaming from Amit's left hand propelled around the room like a deflating party balloon. Petrified, Kenya grabbed his flailing legs but was also carried around the bedroom at great speed, battling to anchor herself in position.

'Control it!' bellowed a sodden Kenya.

'That's not what you were saying earlier!' barked Amit.

'Just relax now. Relax!' yelled Kenya.

Amit focused on calming thoughts. Once again his father came to mind. The waters dwindled to a trickle once more. Slowly, he opened his eyes. The room was dripping in water. The force had been so great that the paint on the ceiling had bubbled, beginning to peel in sympathy with the wallpaper. The squelching underfoot indicated a pool of water underneath which was already resulting in the bowing of the floorboards. Everything that had been arranged on shelves was strewn across the disaster zone.

Amit struggled past the damp squib of Kenya, and with precise control, watered the only dry object in the room – the beleaguered cactus plant.

The live band continued to perform classics from various Bollywood features as a fine drizzle descended from the ceiling. The guests were too occupied by the free cocktail bar and the chattering class opinions on the news of the day to notice. There had been a growing barrage of events – hostilities over borders, strange earth tremors, and the mysterious disappearance of key members of the public. They had even heard that a local churchman, Pastor Brooke, had vanished, adding to the list. The world was at war with itself and everyone had a theory. The working class thought it was a conspiracy to get rid of them, the middle class blamed everyone who looked remotely 'foreign', and the aristocrats were just grateful that they finally had something else to talk about other than polo.

'I think it's definitely the Cold War all over again,' shouted one of the guests.

'What do you expect when they let anyone in to this country?' barked another.

'I think it's the rebalance of the world to its original, true order,' retorted another guest. The chatter died down around him as he wandered through the crowd. He was a slender man with a coarse mane of hair, impeccably attired in a dark grey, tailored suit. No one could place the bewitching man's name or which road he lived on. He walked with such authority that the guests unintentionally cowered as he continued to pass through the silent, rooted throng to the main staircase leading to the first floor.

Kenya had fallen asleep on the bed, piled high with duvets and cushions to give a dry space in the damp room. Amit sat on the soggy edge of the bed, staring at his palms. His left hand appeared untouched from the earlier events but the centre of his right hand had a growing, creeping ache.

Deep in slumber, Kenya felt a growing tightness in her chest, as if her heart was planning to flee. Like prey, she sensed a growing danger lurking in her midst.

'Amit!' screamed Kenya, bolting upright. Her head was pounding and any further words failed to tumble out of her mouth. Before Amit could say anything, the bedroom door was ripped off its hinges. The dark, impeccable stranger stood proudly in the door frame before reverting to his true self.

'Hello. Let me introduce myself. I'm Darkclaw. And I'm a Lycan.'

He launched himself across the room with a snarling bound, his teeth bared ready to sink into the children. With precision, Kenya sent a lightning bolt into the beast's eye, temporarily sending him whimpering away from the bed. There was no time to celebrate. The thundering claws on the staircase told of the arrival of more.

'Think, water! Water!' bellowed Kenya, as she created a shield of light to thwart the beasts' advances.

Amit looked on, panicked. He tried to close down the sounds around him, but the fear that his talent was no use in his hands crept into his mind. Kenya's shield was taking a lot out of her and her body was tiring in front of his eyes. Maybe it was his anger at the attack, or rage at his lack of faith which sent pulsating wave after wave to lash and separate the marauding Lycans. They howled as they were swept crashing down the stairs of the mansion and out onto the manicured lawn.

In all the commotion, the children failed to see a dark being creeping through the broken bedroom window. It was not until the beast stood upright that they registered his terrifying presence. It was Nightfall. Exhausted, Kenya launched a firebolt but missed, and it landed behind the great beast. His huge talons latched onto Amit's flailing right hand. Nightfall swiftly swiped Amit's head, rendering him unconscious, and bounded out with him through a portal that appeared in the bedroom wall.

Broken with fear for her friend, Kenya clutched at her weakened hands that could only fire mere glimmers of light. She collapsed to the sodden floor with a deep, uncontrollable cry.

It was Darshna's howling that awoke him. A pyjama-wearing Milton stumbled out of his bed, remembering to grab his trilby. He always felt more presentable and ready for any mishap in the mansion with his trusted hat firmly placed on his head.

The scene that greeted him was in full contrast to that of the night before. Darshna always threw crazy parties, but Milton shook his head in disbelief at the carnage. Broken glass, food remnants, flood-damaged flooring and muddy animal footprints everywhere – even on the walls. The beautiful people from the night before had gone. All that remained were mascara-streaked faces howling insanely into the comforting arms of police officers and ambulance crews. It was a disaster zone complete with 'Stop Police' tape cordoning off areas.

'No one needs to panic!' panicked Darshna to everyone who passed by her. Her arms flapped around as if controlled by an unseen puppeteer. Her hair, by 'Darren of Mayfair', had evidence from the night terror poking from it. The make-up had long run free of her dripping wet face, leaving colourful track marks from its escape.

Her mud-encrusted sari clung to her heavily, impeding her movement.

'Please, do come again,' she grovelled at a barely conscious Raj Uncle as he was carried out on a stretcher to a waiting ambulance.

'Champagne bar next time! Champagne!' Her wayward arms caused her to lose balance, sending her crashing to the floor.

'Milton, Milton, Milton!' shrieked Darshna, on seeing the driver. Each cry of his name was louder than before, until he was standing over her, helping her to her unsteady feet.

'Look at my beautiful home!' she wailed, clenching her fists. 'I had all the gorgeous people here and it's all ruined! How am I going to live this down? The Kitty Club!'

Fortunately for Milton, Darshna's uncontrollable wailing and gnashing of teeth attracted the attention of a senior police officer and a television crew. Milton's mind was on the children. He left Darshna to her television debut and rushed upstairs to the first floor. The stairway creaked with such volume that Milton feared it might collapse underfoot. Worried by what he would find in Amit's room, he gingerly pushed the door ajar. First thoughts told him the room was empty, until he heard quiet sobbing under a bundle of wet duvets on the bed.

'Girl, what's happened?' he beseeched the tearful Kenya, holding her tight. His caring, sorrowful eyes met the girl's frightened look.

Clutching her bum bag, she cried, 'They have taken Amit, and it's all my fault!'

Chapter 17
Disappeared

Widespread revelry, howling and yelping noises, mixed with the sound of breaking glass, could be heard from the ground entrance to the camp. For weeks a growing thud of marching Lycans had been heard across the area. The camp spirits were high as a crowd gathered around their leader. He stood strong and proud as he addressed his rampaging lessers.

'Tonight we have our prey in our claws. Tomorrow we shall rule!'

The last part of his sentence could barely be heard over the excited wailing from the crowd.

'Darkness shall reign, darkness shall reign!' echoed around the camp.

Hemlock signalled calm.

'Throw your howls to the sky so that all can hear. Our victory is nigh!' Turning to wipe the spittle from his chin, he grabbed the clawed hand of one of his commanders standing in the shadowy background of the makeshift stage.

'I give you your newest commander – Darkclaw!'

The full moon illuminated the beast's face to reveal the impeccable stranger from the night of the party. The fresh markings on his upper arm denoted his new position. The suited beast grinned widely, feigning humility as the baying crowd applauded.

'Others had said it could not be done.' Darkclaw spoke eloquently, giving a long purposeful stare towards Nightfall. 'But I say, with our supreme leader at our side, all things are possible!'

Nightfall grimaced. How quickly all had forgotten it was him who had plucked the human boy from his bedroom.

Darkclaw bowed low to the supreme leader who roared in response, sending a deep shock wave that reverberated throughout the land.

In all the partying that night stood one solitary figure. For the first time, Nightfall's heart clearly spoke to him and reminded him of the Oracle text he had read. It was speaking more than ever and his doubts had returned to haunt him. It told him things he knew but did not want to hear. The rise of Darkclaw would be his own downfall.

Amit's head was held fast in a metal helmet. He gathered that he must have been tethered to the wall for hours. The chains were long and heavy, so that it was a burden to change position. The mud in his once-sodden clothes had baked dry in the heat of his excavated dungeon. A dimly lit candle was the only comfort as shadows danced on the uneven walls. If he could have hung his head down and cried, he would have. Amit thought of all the things that once seemed so important. The right school, the right clothes, the right phone. His mother had taught him well – to be seen with the influential, to eat in the 'happening' restaurants and to fill social media with your jealousy-inspiring pictures. All the effort placed in preparing him to make it in life, to earn lots of money and then, with any luck, to marry lots of money, seemed futile.

He wondered if his mother was okay and wished he could have said all that he wanted to her. The day his father left interrupted his chain of thought once again. He smiled, though, when he thought of Kenya. A heavy sense of calm filled him like never before. Amit placed his head at the maximum angle forward, closed his eyes and prayed that he would not see that flickering candle again.

In the weeks that followed, Kenya spoke of battles, beasts, and the evidence of the Lycans and their meddling in human affairs. She had taken him to see with his own eyes the fate of Dermott and Ardenne, but Milton was still perplexed. He tilted his trilby to the side in order to give his head a good scratch. He often did this when working out a difficult game of dominoes or putting up a shelf. However, no matter how many times he scratched in response to Kenya's tales, he could not find a solution.

'Tell me, child, once more,' he implored Kenya, time and time again. He did not understand, but ignorance was not to stop him from helping Kenya. Milton had accepted years ago that he was not built to understand everything, but if Kenya knew the way to get Amit back, all was fine with him.

It had been a long time since Kenya had felt this safe. Her new home was in a large old outhouse at the end of the garden where Milton lived, undetected by the preoccupied Darshna. Here the old man doted on Kenya like a firstborn grandchild, and she in turn did likewise with him. In the midst of terror around them, Milton had carved out an oasis of calm, whereas the other staff had packed and left to join their frightened families elsewhere. The missing were becoming a large minority, and no family or friendship circle was unaffected. Social services and the police were so inundated with pleas for help that the system buckled under the weight of demand. It was left to individuals to carve out their own safety plans. Kenya was one of the lucky ones with Milton to care for her in her parents' 'absence'. She loved Milton's distracting chatter, but in the pauses of silence she longed for the safe return of Amit.

Milton shuffled to his old television set to lower the volume. The hunt for Amit had seen Darshna on every chat show and newspaper billboard, so her appearance again on daytime TV caused her employee to mute her.

'These rocks. You've got them safe?' asked Milton. He placed two pieces of macaroni pie on the small kitchen table, carefully ensuring Kenya had the largest slice.

'I keep them near me at all times,' replied Kenya, scoffing her pie. 'Amit was protecting me and the amulet. I let him down.' Her voice dropped to a whisper as she remembered her friend's fate. Her appetite dissolved in an instant.

'Don't trouble ya self,' said Milton encouragingly. 'They wanted Amit because they can't touch you!' he explained, emphasising each word by banging his fork on the table. 'I might not understand everything, but I can spot a devilish game plan a mile off!' he proudly added.

Kenya sat up in the wake of Milton's confidence.

'It's a trap?' she asked, looking earnestly at the old man.

'Of course!' exclaimed Milton. 'They know you are going to look for Amit. They will expect to bargain with you for his return.'

'That's a risk on their part. Who's to say I would exchange the amulet pieces for Amit?'

Though she spoke defiantly, neither she nor Milton believed her last words.

'They know, because you would,' replied Milton. In the background, Darshna's tearful pleas on the muted television looked like a dramatic scene from a silent movie.

'They know you two only have each other,' he added quietly, staring blankly at Darshna's continued appeal.

Chapter 18
The Camp

The View had been devoid of humans for a while, since the unexplained disappearance of ramblers and dog walkers. Any brave souls who remained left after a convoy of soldiers in armoured vehicles failed to return from patrolling the area. Night after night, various Lycans had flocked through the numerous tunnels to the underground camp to pay allegiance to Hemlock. Above ground, the world's discord was growing by the hour whilst the majority of humans remained apathetic, plugged into their technology. Hemlock mused that the takeover would be easier than he had thought. Stupid humans! He felt the expectant power raging through his veins, making him more terrible, more unbearable than before.

He was not the only beast growing in power. Commander after commander was replaced, propelling the conniving Darkclaw further along the chain of command. Praise was heaped on him to the extent that he and his growing entourage could do what they pleased within the camp. At times, the lesser beasts were more fearful of his merciless claw than that of the impulsive supreme leader.

The sounding of the evening conch signalled the gathering of the high commanders. Nightfall's fearsome pace was replaced with a reluctant shuffle as he passed through the camp to the Command Hut. His heart would not be silenced. It was not happy, and nor was Nightfall.

'My liege,' addressed Nightfall as he entered the hut. Already present were his weakened commanders, and Darkclaw. The stripes on the cunning Lycan indicated that he had been freshly promoted once again.

'How nice of you to drop in!' drooled Darkclaw sarcastically. The room filled with nervous laughter from desperate commanders eager to keep their positions – and their heads. Darkclaw continued to file his dark talons without looking up as he acknowledged Nightfall. He purposefully lounged across the large chair normally assigned to Nightfall, daring him to make a remark or a challenge. Nightfall stared down at the young pretender. Darkclaw was wearing an eclectic mix of recent spoils – combat fatigues taken from the failed army patrol, a Barbour walking jacket and an Armani scarf worn neatly as a cravat.

'You impertinent imbecile!' snarled Nightfall as he launched himself at the grinning upstart. Red rage engulfed him before he could remember where he was. Hemlock stepped stealthily from the shadows.

'This so-called "imbecile" is the new commander in charge of daily operations. Your failures and excuses have cost us time.' Hemlock spoke with restrained anger that made the spines on Nightfall's wide back rise. 'The boy still sleeps,' he added, growling.

'I'm… I'm sorry. My liege, no one can wake the boy,' explained Nightfall. His every word was met with the widening of Darkclaw's smile. 'He seems to be in some kind of trance or bewitchment.'

'I am absolute power!' interrupted Hemlock. 'There is no power greater than mine!' His booming rant rumbled throughout the camp, causing all who heard it to wince in fear.

'The great Oracle foretells all. Wake the boy and find that girl's weak point. Like all pathetic humans, she will seek to rescue him. We will strike a deal – the boy in exchange for the fragment pieces.'

'We'll give him back in pieces, for the pieces!' added Darkclaw dryly.

Chapter 19
Chained

This was like no other sleep. The point at which consciousness began and ended were blurred. The guards had tried everything to awaken Amit, but he merely sighed deeply and fell further into his slumber world: a deep, peaceful rest, cradled in the protective arms of another. Amit saw himself fleetingly as a young boy, laughing with his father. A voice from the protective arms spoke quietly, but he could only hear a muffled sound. He leaned forward to hear more.

'They are coming to harm you,' whispered the voice. 'They are coming to harm you!'

This time the voice was more urgent. Slithers of light crept under Amit's eyelids. He blinked several times before he saw the outline of the monstrous beast from his nightmares. The beast that had clawed Kenya. Before he could recoil in fear, he spotted the gentleness in Nightfall's eyes. The oppressive chains were broken in a matter of minutes by Nightfall's hefty claws. He continued to free Amit in silence, concentrating on the task at hand. Amit sat in awe of the terrifying beast gently kneeling before him. It was Nightfall who broke the silence.

'You've been in a deep trance since your arrival. They are desperate to awaken you to gain information on the girl. Your supreme leader must have been watching over you!'

'I... I don't have a supreme leader,' stuttered Amit, moving his stiff arms and legs freely.

'We all have a supreme leader,' responded Nightfall swiftly and with conviction Amit decided not to contest him.

The rugged Lycan gingerly lifted the metal helmet that was locked firmly onto Amit's head. It was heavily embossed with ancient symbols and patterns.

'It is used to stop you connecting to your talent,' said Nightfall, as if he were reading Amit's thoughts. Amit stared at his freed hands and began to clear his mind. He could feel a cold stream coursing through his body from his feet upwards to his hands. He would have successfully released a flood of water from his palm if it had not been for the Lycan.

'Don't do that here!' barked Nightfall. 'In an instant these mud walls would collapse in water – with you trapped in here!'

He helped a shaky Amit to his feet, who clung to his armoured side like a father welcoming a prodigal son.

Chapter 20
Battle Cry

Milton's life had been eventful because of the presence of strong women in his life. He knew Kenya would grow into a fine one as he drove through the abandoned streets of Harrow. The intermittent street lights and the downed live electrical cables scattered across the roads made such trips perilous. Milton steadily avoided the large potholes that had been made by the marauding beasts exiting the underworld. They had terrorised the country in search of mischief.

A hurried state of emergency had been declared earlier that day across social media. The police and army had been decimated by heavy defeats and desertion, making the strict curfews unenforceable. Those who could afford to had already left for safer places abroad, leaving those left behind in perpetual fear and distrust of others. The law had become 'do whatever you can to survive'.

'Have you ever been really scared, Uncle Milton?' Kenya spoke quietly, staring at the destruction filing past the car window.

Milton scratched his head thoughtfully before answering. 'It's normal to be nervous in new situations. Remember, though, this is a different time. It is pointless being scared of what you can't control.'

Kenya's puzzled look forced him to continue.

'Look at all this!' he shouted, angrily pointing at the destruction beyond. 'Made by fear! No one defending the defenceless, because of fear.'

'Bad things happen when good people do nothing,' replied Kenya. 'I remember reading something like that on a poster in class.'

'That's my girl!' boomed Milton, brimming with pride.

Guards were mounted at the main entrance to the underworld with strict instructions to inform the supreme leader of any sightings of humans. Lesser worker beasts patrolled nervously around the perimeter of the area, on the edge of the surrounding woods. Their talk was of a magical human girl with untold powers who could defeat Hemlock.

Unknown to them, their greatest enemy was a few hundred metres away, sheltering under shrubbery with an old man. Kenya and Milton had come with such urgency without a definite plan of action, apart from not getting caught. It was so silent that each could hear the other's breathing, as clear as a church bell on a still morning. Kenya's heart was pounding furiously, but Milton signalled with his hands for her to calm down. This was not the time to talk.

The deafening silence was broken by the low hum emitting from the amulet pieces strapped to Kenya's waist under her jumper. She tried in vain to muffle the increasing noise, to no avail. In the commotion to silence the pieces, Kenya and Milton failed to hear the crunching of dry twigs on the forest floor or the thrashing of leaves to clear the path ahead. A muscular clawed hand slowly gripped Kenya and Milton tightly around their mouths. They tried to struggle free but it caused the grip to be stronger.

When Milton opened his eyes, he closed them again straight away. He could not trust his senses. Opening them once more, he confirmed that he had truly gone mad. Crouching before him was a proud beast, who he guessed when standing upright was at least two metres in height. The creature had the old man's trusty trilby in its claws. That was a step too far for Milton.

'Get ya own hat!' he snapped at Nightfall, who was taken aback by the ferocity.

'Milton, it's OK. He's on our side!'

It was a voice Milton knew as well as his very own.

'Amit, my boy!' Milton pushed past Nightfall and grabbed Amit in a bear hug.

The Lycan seemed curious to observe the mutual back slapping and Milton's need to rub Amit's head periodically. The strange customs were not shared by the girl, who broke free from the hugging to stare long and hard at Nightfall's fearsome talons.

'How do we know if we can trust him?' Kenya's harsh tone flattened Milton's and Amit's ongoing celebrations.

'He helped me escape, Kenya,' explained Amit.

'He tried to kill me! I have the scars to prove that,' replied Kenya.

Amit could see distrust in her eyes as he beckoned Nightfall to speak.

'The supreme leader is hoping you'll try to rescue Amit. He would offer a deal to ensure that he would have the amulet pieces and both of you out of the way forever.'

'We need his help.' Amit's plea to Kenya was interrupted by a booming roar rising from the camp in the distance. The ground shook violently with the sound of galloping hooves and claws leaping out of the mouth of the enemy's lair.

'I think he has found out you've escaped!' exclaimed Milton.

'Take cover, brave one,' replied Nightfall. He gently lifted the protesting man high into the air, placing him safe in the canopy of a great oak tree.

Kenya took a deep breath. It was time. She opened the small bum bag around her waist, returning Amit's amulet piece to its protector. The piece chimed a soothing tune as if to welcome Amit back. Without words, Amit placed it safely in an inside pocket close to his heart. The third piece vibrated greatly, beseeching for the protection of its owner. The vibrations reverberated through Nightfall uncontrollably, as both he and the lonely piece sang out in perfect harmony. Amit held out his hand to Kenya, who reluctantly placed the third amulet piece in his palm.

'This is yours,' Amit spoke solemnly to Nightfall, placing the piece firmly in the beast's large claw. 'Fight to protect it.'

'No! It cannot be!' protested Nightfall, fighting to place the piece back in Amit's hands. 'The guardians must be Children of Gabriel, Angel Sapiens. The very look of me, my very presence speaks of beast. I'm not worthy of such honour.'

The great beast's face was long with sorrow and past regrets. As he continued to argue that his people were the forbidden race, the amulet piece continued to sing a contradictory tune within his clasped claws.

'You belong with us, Nightfall. It's your heart that makes you a Child of Gabriel, not your outward appearance.' Amit was puzzled by how for once he had found the right words to say.

Humbled, Nightfall placed the amulet piece in a pocket on his belt without further protest. Surely, the human part of their brain had caused an error? Everything he had been taught from his cub days disintegrated right before his eyes. The Great had installed in him a deep hatred for humans, and especially those few Angel Sapiens who were left. None of their kind was to be spared, but erased from the surface of this earth. In that moment, Nightfall knew that all that he had taken as truth was far from it. The whole purpose of his life had been a lie, for here before him were two children willing to see past his breeding. The weight of his past life laid heavy on his shoulders as he hung his head low.

Kenya turned away; she knew within her that Amit was right, but she wrestled with her logical mind that distrusted the beast. Gaining composure, she turned to look at Nightfall.

'You are the guardian of the earth. Place your trust in it and it will release the talent through you.'

'Fight to protect your amulet piece,' added Amit, patting Nightfall's mighty arms. In return, Nightfall gave a short nod in reply before joining Kenya's gaze at the horizon. The three faced the growing thunder of the oncoming army, coming closer with every heartbeat. Emptying their minds, they stood and waited.

Though they were only three fighting back a mighty wall of evil, it felt like they had the power of many on their side. As Milton watched on, a heavy scent of sweet lavender engulfed him. As he fought his own battle against his heavy eyelids, he thought he saw an unseen army of thousands fighting alongside the three. With a feeling of true peace, he fell into a deep trance, as if in the arms of another. As he dreamt, the battle raged on.

Nightfall proved to be a skilful fighter, protecting the children with his brute strength as they wielded their fledgling talents. His heart continued to sing in tune with his amulet piece as he sent the attackers flying backwards in all directions.

Kenya's lightning reflex sent the lesser-skilled Lycans running for cover. The smell of singed fur and charred spines stopped a number of the less brave hurtling forward. Incredible jets of high-pressure water pummelled the hardy warriors out of the area as Amit summoned all his energy through his left hand. Occasionally, Amit's water would clash with Kenya's lightning, causing sparks and secondary fires to break out near the camp entrance where the elite Lycans stood watching.

Hemlock's mood grew thick with hatred as he saw his former commander standing tall next to the 'mere humans'. Darkclaw's jealousy of Nightfall being so close to the powerful amulet pieces grew exponentially. His dark thoughts were disturbed by the supreme leader.

'Call out the reserves!' he yelled.

'But, sire! The camp will be left unprotected,' replied a guard who dared to respond. Hemlock grabbed the hapless soldier by the throat.

'I said, I want them all out here and I want them here now!' he growled, before throwing the guard to the ground like a piece of rubbish.

'I think we can do that and more, my liege,' replied Darkclaw, mysteriously.

The battle grew weary but the three could see fewer and fewer forces coming forward. Soon it was nothing more than a trickle of lesser beasts who fled at the very sight of an angry-looking Kenya coming into focus. Wringing her tired hands, Kenya looked across at the kneeling Nightfall who had slumped forward onto the churned earth in front of him; his heavy, rapid breathing told how hard and spiritedly he had fought. His amulet piece gave a soothing purr as if to comfort its battle-worn owner.

The mottled sky opened up as if the lull in the fighting was a signal. The view became a spectacular lightning display to rival Kenya's efforts. Each flash of lightning revealed the deep wounds on Nightfall's body. The rain that followed dropped like silver darts, adding to the misery of such a cold night.

It was the dapper Darkclaw who first came into Kenya's view, followed by Hemlock. Anger over the night's events had increased his ferocity and size to even greater proportions.

'This is his talent,' muttered a sombre Nightfall. His forlorn expression was so great that Amit felt compelled to help the great beast to his feet. The tenderness of someone so small pleased Nightfall's heart immensely.

'Well done. Well done, mere mortal girl,' growled Hemlock. He anchored an ornate silver spear to the ground and began a deafening round of slow clapping. The sound echoed menacingly around the View.

'Having three amulet pieces could not help you,' Darkclaw joined in. His clearly spoken words were laced with sarcasm. 'Needed the help from a turncoat, a traitor, a non-entity!'

His smugness was insufferable even for Kenya, who was still not wholly convinced about Nightfall. Amit, however, stood in front of the crestfallen beast as if to shield him from further verbal venom. Darkclaw's words evoked more menace within Hemlock, who growled with such demonic ferocity that the force flattened weakened trees, and dead branches were sent crashing to the ground.

'Give me what belongs to me,' commanded Hemlock. 'I and only I know the true powers that the amulet can unlock!'

'They are not yours or anyone's to unlock,' Kenya spoke with such poise that Amit's nerves were steadied.

'What is this that thinks it can defy me?' snarled Hemlock. 'I will scatter you and your people like you were straw!'

Kenya could see the approval in Nightfall's eyes as she stood up to his former master.

'My name is Kenya and I will always defy you.' Kenya's voice cut through the night air like a samurai sword. What fears Nightfall had for his future were severed from his body.

Kenya stared directly at Hemlock. She would have remained rooted to the ground if the conniving Darkclaw had not cleared his throat.

'Maybe, sire, I could suggest a deal which will see all parties... happier.' A sly grin filled his face.

'The amulet pieces hold untold riches and power. You would be able to reverse whatever wrongs you decide. You could change the course of history, make your life fulfilled... even bring back loved ones.' As he spoke, Kenya could see a slight twitch in Amit's face. Darkclaw pressed on. 'You could bring those you love back together. Imagine what changes that would make for your poor mother, Darshna.'

'Don't listen to him!' shouted Kenya. She could feel Amit slipping, losing his grip, lowering his guard.

'All those years of being a disappointment to your mother would simply vanish. You could be the one who brings your family together again,' persuaded Darkclaw. Kenya was drawn to his honeyed voice, laden with soothing tones. Her mind hung on every compelling word.

'Or bring back your father and grandmother, dear girl.' Kenya felt Darkclaw's penetrating stare within her, as if his claws had encircled her mind.

'Humans perceive us as mere mythical half-breeds consigned to folklore. But we have talents that could see us rise and take over this land for ourselves. Our rightful inheritance!'

Amit's hand was on his amulet piece. He thought of his father and the 'hows' and the 'what ifs' that occupied space in his mind.

'We're the same,' purred Darkclaw. 'We have the same blood coursing through our veins. It is our destiny, our right to use our talents to further our kind. No more living in the shadows of the dark.'

'Let's share our talents, and make this world ours,' added Hemlock.

A heavy, sweet scent had fallen on Kenya. Her mind was elsewhere, filled with childhood wants and fading memories. She looked through hazy eyes to see that the amulet pieces were now in both her and Amit's palms.

'Custodians cannot give what is not theirs to give. We are here to guard, and this is what we must do.' Kenya heard Nightfall's calm words travel through the fog that was her mind.

'On guard!' Kenya heard the cry tumble out of her own mouth. Out of the deep wooded cover came the remaining baying hordes. Kenya sent bolt upon bolt raining down on the Lycan masses. The supreme leader quickly surrounded himself with the lesser beasts, who he used as sacrificial protection from the onslaught. Awoken from his thoughts, Amit sent streams of beast warriors down the sides of the View in torrents of water.

The battle was more ferocious than it had been before. Kenya could sense her body weakening under the intensity. Either side of her were Amit and Nightfall.

'Whatever happens, you must carry on.' Her eyes spoke the unsaid to her companions.

'It is my duty,' replied Nightfall solemnly. As soon as the words were uttered, his amulet piece became a bright light from which all had to turn their eyes. With a great cry, he hit his mighty fists against the sodden earth, causing the ground to shake. Beast after beast fell into the growing chasm as the earth opened up in front of them. A roar from the supreme leader sent Kenya hurtling to the ground as he and his gathered beasts marched towards her. Dazed from the fall and weakened by the battle, she saw the looming supreme leader armed with the ornate silver spear.

'This one is mine,' he growled to his warriors as he held the spear aloft. Kenya closed her weary eyes and waited for the inevitable.

An earth-shuddering quake rattled through the View. A gap appeared behind Hemlock and his entourage. A deluge of water engulfed the warriors, sending them downwards into the chasm. Hemlock's claws and his spear grappled in the mud of the gully until he was close to the top of the slippery opening. In the distance, he could see the hated Nightfall, the turncoat, guarding the fallen Kenya. The outline of Darkclaw came into focus.

'My liege,' Darkclaw addressed him politely. He grabbed the silver spear from his leader's grip. With one claw raised in anticipation of being pulled up to safety, the supreme leader snapped his fingers impatiently at his commander.

'Oh, sorry, my liege,' replied Darkclaw, before swiftly pushing Hemlock down into the blackness below.

'No hard feelings!' he shouted downwards, smiling, wiping his claws free of mud. He turned without a care and strode towards Kenya with the spear held aloft. To little avail she fired off a series of lightning bolts towards him. Grinning, Darkclaw hurled the silver spear deep into Nightfall's back as he shielded Kenya with his body. The laughter of Darkclaw scurrying off was coupled with the heavy thud of Nightfall's body against the muddy ground. Last remnants of beasts were washed away to the bottom of the View or into the many crevices that dotted the area. The area returned to silence once more.

The great beast lay on the ground with his life force draining from him. Amit cradled Nightfall's head in his lap. Thoughts criss-crossed Kenya's mind of all the events that had led to this moment. The more she felt pity for the fallen creature, the more the scars on her arm sought to remind her that he had once been an enemy. A hum from the amulet pieces descended on the scene.

'We have to do something!' yelled Amit to Kenya. There were too few people who cared for him in his life and he was not prepared to let this one go. Nightfall's great chest moved laboriously as he gasped for breath. Using the last of his strength, he grabbed Amit's arm. Nightfall looked deep into Amit's eyes as if to register his friend's face one last time. His body trembled as it fought to stay alive, and his eyes closed.

'I'm not going to let him die!' exclaimed Amit. As he spoke, a trickle appeared from his right hand. It glowed as it coursed from his hand down Nightfall's face. Slowly, Nightfall's eyes opened as the water revived him.

'Look! It's healing him!' exclaimed Kenya. She pushed back her negative thoughts and concentrated her effort to produce a slender controlled beam from her right palm. Frightened of what it might do to the fallen beast, she gingerly illuminated a patch of earth on the ground next to Nightfall. Immediately, small sprigs of ground-hugging heather began to sprout, covering the small patch. Gingerly, she raised her hand and allowed the soft beam to cover Nightfall. For a while nothing seemed to change. At the point of giving up, Nightfall shut his eyes and let out a whimper. Gradually, the numerous spear and talon wounds faded away until his body was as robust and strong as ever. He tentatively opened his eyes to see Kenya. Sheepishly, she looked away from his gaze. The girl he had tried to kill had helped to heal him. Before him was everything he had been taught to hate. He had been saved by the enemy. He stretched out his great clawed hand into which Kenya placed her small hand, and she guided the Lycan to his feet. Upright in front of the young human, he bowed low in front of her and was rewarded with the most heartfelt hug from both the children.

'Thank you, Light Child,' he whispered into Kenya's ear.

They surveyed the nightmare scene of the earlier battle before them. Beyond the churned, gaping earth were small pinpricks of light in the distance, where electricity was still present across North London. The feeling of winning the battle but not yet the war sprung to Kenya's mind. There were still too many questions to be asked.

'We should head to your home first,' said Amit wearily. 'You will be able turn your parents back to normal in due course.'

The look on Kenya's face told of the fear the normality of her parents evoked.

'We have more control of our gifts now,' reassured Amit.

'And what of Darkclaw? Will he be back?' asked Kenya. She already knew the answer but hoped that Nightfall's expression would tell her otherwise. The great Lycan's eyes confirmed her worry.

'At least he did not get the amulet pieces. We still have those,' smiled Amit encouragingly.

'You both did well, young humans. Very well.' Nightfall spoke with such pride that it touched the children. 'There is still much to be aware of. Only pure silver can kill our kind,' he explained, holding the muddy silver spear. 'Many of the Lycan and the other Nephanaks will lie in the ground, reforming to spring forth again,' he added.

154

Milton remained asleep in his lavender dreams, as Nightfall slung him over his broad shoulders. The children walked on either side of the Lycan along the silent, deserted roads back to Amit's home.

'When they come back, we will be more than ready,' said a steadfast Kenya. She smiled, gripping Nightfall's large clawed hand firmly.

The Aftermath

The world order quickly settled back into its former rhythm. Conspiracy theories raged across social media as politicians quashed rumours of rampaging beasts, agreeing it was a highly coordinated human attack. A few of the disappeared returned, dazed and unable to recall their ordeal. Many more, including Pastor Brooke, were never seen again – just casualties of another war. No definite explanation could be given as to why the epicentre of the destruction was a small area in London. Fears were quelled as all efforts were made to prevent such attacks happening again. Bills passed through the damaged Parliament aimed to watch out for the 'unknown enemy'. Treaties were signed, cities rebuilt and there was great optimism in the air.

Within a couple of months that 'night of terror' was old news, to be replaced by new celebrity gossip. This was good news for Darshna. She had found fame as a television presenter during Amit's disappearance. Now her Kitty Club was the envy of London, televised weekly to the masses. Luckily, her team of advisors assured her that her revenue and popularity would not be affected by Amit's return. Thus, she agreed to star in a documentary showing their tearful reunion and to speak publicly about his rescue from 'the hands of gunmen wearing wolf masks'. Her mansion continued to be managed by Milton and a small number of staff as she fluttered from one exclusive interview to the next. Unknown to her was the biggest 'scoop' of her life – the true identity of her new, rugged groundsman. During the day, Nightfall shapeshifted to work in the garden around the large house. His evenings were spent in a new extension to Milton's home at the bottom of the garden. Here, Milton spent many an hour educating the Lycan on the finer points of human life, which in Milton's case was dominoes and horse racing.

As Darshna carved out her new career, Amit spent his free time honing his new talent under Nightfall's knowledgeable tutorage. For Kenya, her weeks continued as before, slaving hard for her ungrateful parents. She thought long and hard about the benefits of leaving her parents in their frozen state. With a reluctant heart, she knew it would cause suspicion amongst the neighbours if her parents were not seen.

However, the return to normality did not bring Ardenne much joy. When Adosia's last will and testament was finally read, Kenya became the sole heir, as expected. Unfortunately for her greedy parents, the money was locked away in a trust until Kenya's 18th birthday. Ardenne was left with the prospect of spending more years than she wished with Dermott, waiting on the promise of a lion's share of his mother's fortunes. To add to their stress, both Ardenne and Dermott suffered with severe memory loss. Doctors had no idea what was the cause of their problems. Kenya, however, knew the reason: she would return them to their previous frozen state whenever their demands became too much, or when she wanted to visit Amit and Milton.

Friday nights were special to Amit and Kenya: they were reserved for Milton's campfire and Nightfall's tales of life underground. Kenya loved the time spent with the gentle beast and sang him songs learned from her grandmother as she warmed herself by the fire. It was on one of these occasions she watched him lumber to the end of the garden. Here, he stood majestically with his face raised upwards towards the heavens.

Kenya nudged Amit as they sat by the fire, pointing at the lonely figure in the distance. Milton was deep in concentration, placing alternate cubes of meat and vegetables on skewers. Quietly, the children got up and joined the stargazing creature. He greeted them with a nod before returning his attention to the skies. Kenya leaned her tired head against Nightfall's arm.

'Can you see something?' questioned Kenya, gazing upwards.

Nightfall surveyed the midnight blue skies as if he could read a message hidden in the positioning of the stars.

'I feel them regrouping, Light Child. They'll come soon. It's only the hour that we do not know,' Nightfall spoke so sadly that Amit held his hand.

'We will defeat them again!' reassured Amit. His voice was sure and strong.

'We have been practising our talents every day. We'll be ready,' added Kenya. She had gained an unshakeable confidence since the night of the battle which had penetrated every aspect of her being.

Nightfall smiled. 'You are a lioness, Light Child! A true Child of Gabriel. We will need all your courage to find the other amulet pieces.'

It was Kenya and Amit's turn to stargaze as Nightfall looked on Milton stoking the fire in the distance.

'Somewhere out there are others like us,' Amit smiled. The stars twinkled in agreement with the onlooking admirers below.

'It is our duty. We will find them and the lost fragments.' Kenya looked at her friends. Without arrogance, her voice was matter of fact, as if it was already a done deal. There was no hint of compromise or the prospect of failure.

'You are right, brave one. We will find them,' agreed Nightfall.

He stared down at the young human. She was not tall or fierce nor physically strong for the arduous journey ahead. There was no great presence to be seen, but she had something indescribable. Nightfall concluded that the human child's supreme leader had made an excellent choice. Amit also looked at his friend. The moonlight had highlighted the steely, determined expression on her face that he had grown accustomed to.

'At least we have each other,' concluded Kenya. She gripped Nightfall's clawed hand firmly as they walked back to the campfire.

The night continued with laughter between the children and hearty food from Milton. Nightfall looked on at his new human family with a growing sense of pride and a desire to protect them. Kenya noted that he did not sing with her songs, or tell his stories of old. She leaned against his arm and left him to be silent in thought. However, in the midnight blue of that night, Nightfall's heart sang songs of the children's bravery and shone throughout the darkness like a black diamond.